ZAC

MIXOLOGY SERIES

KRISSY V

ZAC

Everyone thinks they know Zac James, but no-one actually really does. He likes to think that he's pretty much an enigma. After being broken-hearted once, he learned to keep his heart closed to others. Now he's on a path of self-destruction and there will be hell to play if anyone gets in the way.

Isabella Todd (Issy) is a party girl with a serious attitude. She knows what she wants, and she won't stop until she gets it. Unfortunately, she has Zac in her line of sight.

Watch this toxic relationship spiral out of control, as two big ego's fight for control.

Can Zac fight his demons one last time and can Issy let someone else rule her heart?

Mum, you are a fighter. You astound me with your strength to keep going.
Love you loads.

Contents

PROLOGUE

Where the fuck is she?

Erika is a designer; sometimes she gets carried away with a project and doesn't realise what time it is. She's always late for our dates. It makes me mad. But I just can't stay mad at her for long. I love Erika. She's my soulmate and I would do anything for her.

I work in London, at one of the large banks. My job is really stressful, so I always liked to play hard. However, since I met Erika and she moved in with me, the only playing I like to do is with her. It's our anniversary today and we've been together for three happy years.

I'm particularly eager for her to finish work tonight because I'm going to ask her to marry me. My beautiful, elegant, Erika, the love of my life, and I can't wait to show her the ring I have to seal the deal. It's a huge, square diamond with smaller diamonds running down the neck of the platinum ring. Taking it out of my pocket, I look at it one more time, just to make sure I haven't dropped it on the way here. Yep, it's still there. I put it back in my pocket, knowing the next time I take it out will be when I put it on her finger.

Having been a bit wild since I moved to London, I never thought I would settle down. I've been earning a lot of money working in the banking industry. It's high-pressured, so we let off a lot of steam after work. That meant drinks, drugs, and women. Lots of women.

I met Erika on one of those many nights out and she changed my perspective on relationships. She showed me how good it can be with someone you love.

Checking my phone one more time, I throw it down on the table because she still hasn't messaged me. I can feel my anger rising through my body. She had better not have totally forgotten about tonight. I'm nervous and frustrated at the same time.

Dialling her number for the fourth time, I put the phone to my ear, ready to hear her excuses. It rings and rings. No answer.

"Excuse me, sir. Do you want a drink while you're waiting?" someone says, breaking through my thoughts.

"Please. I think I'm going to need one. Can I have a bottle of sauvignon blanc, the most expensive you have, please, and a Courvoisier."

He nods and moves away from the table.

Picking up the phone again, I ring her number. She'd better answer this time.

"Hello… Zac, I'm sorry." She sounds out of breath. "I was just handing some work over. I know I'm running late, but I'm on my way. I'm just locking up now." She's panting, so I know she's moving fast.

"Erika, just hurry up, will you? I'm sitting her like a tit waiting for you. Everyone is looking at me like I've been stood up and you know how much that pisses me off. I wanted tonight to be special."

"I know, Zac, and I'm sorry. I'll make it up to you later, I promise," she says seductively.

A smile spreads across my face. "How are you going to make it up to me, baby?" We love playing this game. Because we both work long hours, sometimes we sext each other. It keeps our relationship alive and it's great fun.

I can picture her smiling as she says, "Well, the first thing I'm going to do is reach under the table and feel your cock, give it a squeeze, and then I'm going to take my pants off and put them in my pocket. You're going to have sit while we have dinner and know I'm wet and ready for you."

"Erika, you're killing me."

"I'm going to do a lot more than that."

"I want you to tell me when you're in the back of the taxi."

"But he'll hear me," she says.

"Yeah, I know, and that will turn me on even more. You owe me. I'm sitting here in this posh restaurant, on my own, waiting for the love of my life with a massive, hard cock."

She laughs. I love that laugh. It makes me so happy. "Okay, I'm all locked up, lover boy. I'm coming to get you. Hang on, there's a taxi. I'm just going to put my hand up and grab it."

"That sounds like you're talking about my cock." I laugh.

"Wait a few more minutes, big boy."

I hear her shout, "Taxi!" then I hear her running in her high heels.

All of a sudden, I hear horns beeping, a scream, and people shouting all at once.

"Fuck, Erika. What's going on?" Nothing. Erika is the

type of person who would stop and help someone if they fell over or needed some help.

"Erika!" I shout again. I stand up and walk outside the restaurant. I don't want to be shouting for her attention in the middle of the place.

"Erika, tell me what's going on. Erika!"

I hear a commotion on the other end of the phone. Someone says, "Ring an ambulance. She's in a bad way."

My heart starts racing and I scream down the phone. "For fuck's sake, Erika! Answer the phone!" I need to know that my forever girl is okay and she's just helping someone else out.

There's some more shuffling and I keep calling her name. Next thing I hear the noises that someone is picking up the phone as if they had dropped it..

"Erika," I say, relieved to hear her moving. "What's going on? Are you okay?"

"Excuse me, who is this?"

My heart drops.

"Where's Erika? Put her on the phone. Tell her I'm losing my life here. She's about five foot nine, she has brunette hair and she's ..."

"I'm sorry, there was an accident. She's not able to come to the phone. Who are you?"

"I'm her partner. What the fuck is going on?" I'm screaming down the phone now.

"She's been knocked over." The voice speaks with no empathy whatsoever.

"What? Oh my God, put her on the phone so I can talk to her. I can calm her down. I bet she's panicking."

"I'm sorry, sir…" I hear some voices in the background and the sirens have stopped. It takes another couple of minutes before someone takes the phone and says, "Are you her boyfriend?"

"Yes, I am. Can you tell me what the fuck is going on?" I'm getting to the point where I'm going to explode if they don't put Erika on the phone.

"Sir. Calm down. She's been involved in an accident and the ambulance is here. They're going to take her to St. George's Hospital."

"I'm on my way."

"Sir, it's not looking good."

"What the fuck does that mean? I don't care if she's broken a leg or something."

"No, sir. Prepare yourself for the worst. We are prepping her ready to leave. Hurry and meet us there." He hangs up.

What the fuck does he mean, 'prepare for the worst'? She was crossing a road, for fuck's sake. The cars don't move fast at this time of night.

I jump into a cab and ask him to get to the hospital quickly.

I feel sick. My heart is pounding. I'm clammy. I just don't know what's going on. The traffic is heavy, so I get out of the taxi and run the rest of the way. When I run into the hospital A&E, I can hardly breathe. "I'm here to see Erika Williams. She was brought in by ambulance."

The receptionist checks her computer screen. "Can you wait over there please, sir? Someone will be out to see you shortly."

I sit down where she tells me to and start tapping my foot, waiting for someone to tell me what the fuck is going on. It only takes a couple of minutes for someone to come out, but it feels like forever.

"Sir? Are you waiting to see Erika Williams?"

"Yes, I am," I say, standing. "Where is she?"

"Are you her husband? Brother?"

"I'm her boyfriend. Well, fiancé."

"Do you know how to contact her family?"

"Can you just tell me what's going on? Then I can call her family."

"Well, you're not really a relative."

"I'm the only one here. I was going to ask her to marry me tonight. We live together. What more do you want to know? How many times a week we have sex? I can give you that information if you want." He is starting to really piss me off.

"That's fine. Come with me and I'll take you to her."

"Finally," I say under my breath, although I guess it was loud enough that he heard me because he turns to face me and then keeps walking.

He stops outside a cubicle and I can hear a lot of commotion behind the curtain. "She's in here." I start to reach for the curtain, but he stops me. "Before you go in, she's in a bad way. We're trying to stop the internal bleeding, but we need to operate. We need you to sign the paperwork."

"What do you mean *she's in a bad way*? I don't care what she looks like. I love her. I just want this nightmare to be over."

He pulls back the curtain and I nearly vomit. My beautiful Erika is laid on the table with her top in ribbons. Her bra has been cut open and everyone can see her tits. Well, actually, they can't, because there's so much blood on her body that you can't see it's her. She has tubes everywhere. She's hooked up to some machines that are beeping. There are lots of people in this small cubicle and they're all busy.

I stumble backwards and the doctor is behind me.

"Are you okay?"

"What's happening in here?" I manage to say. I feel dizzy and sick.

"We're about to move her into theatre. She has a

ruptured spleen, some broken bones, and there is a lot of bleeding, but we can't work out where it's coming from. We need to open her up and see if we can stop the bleeding."

"Do whatever you have to do to save her," I plead, almost falling to my knees.

"We will. I promise. The paperwork is ready for you and we will take you to a private room where you can wait. We'll let you know what's happening. You need to ring her family though. They need to know what's going on."

"I'll… I'll do that now."

I watch them wheel her out of the cubicle and I stop them. "Let me talk to her for one minute. Please?"

"Okay, but you need to hurry up. We need to operate immediately."

I stand close to her and touch her face. I don't care about the blood on my hands. It's part of Erika. "Baby, I love you. I was going to ask you to marry me tonight." I have to hold back my tears. "You could have just said no. You didn't have to go to this extent to avoid it." I take her hand in between mine and squeeze it and bring it to my mouth. "When you're better, I'm going to ask you again, but Erika, will you be my wife?"

I kiss her on the lips and feel my tears drip off my face onto her bloodstained face.

"I'm sorry, we really need to go."

"Bye, baby. See you soon." I cry as they wheel her away and into the theatre.

A nurse comes and shows me into the private waiting area and I sit in the chair and sob. I know I have to ring her family, but I can't face it. Picking up my phone, I ring the only person I know who can help me.

It rings three times before I hear her voice.

"Mum, I need you," I say before I sob uncontrollably down the phone.

WHAT'S YOUR
NAME AGAIN?

1 ½ OZ GIN, 1 ½ OZ LEMON JUICE, ¾ OZ ORANGE
CURACAO, ¾ OZ CHERRY LIQUER, LEMON-LIME SODA,
TO TOP

FIVE YEARS LATER

It's Friday night and Mixology is jam packed. As far as
I'm concerned, it's another night, another dollar. I work as
much as I can; not for the money, but because it keeps me
out of trouble. Although, admittedly, recently I've started
to sink back into my old ways. If any of my family found
out, they would kill me.

Tonight is not a good night. It's been five years to the
day since I lost Erika. I know when I finish here there is
only one place I'm going. The Underground.

"The queue is around the corner, Zac," Ainsley says.
"It's gonna be busy."

"It always is on a Friday night. Nothing new there."

"How you doing?" she asks, looking at me with sad

9

eyes. I hate when she looks at me like that. Actually, I hate anyone looking at me sympathetically; it makes me feel weak.

"Fine," I answer gruffly.

"Guess you don't want to talk about it, as usual." She opens the door to let the next group of people in.

As she talks to the group of girls, I hear a voice coming through my earpiece. "Zac, we need you by the toilets. Shit going down."

"Got to go, Ains," I say, before opening the door and heading into the masses. The music hits me as soon as I walk in. Skylar is playing some amazing tunes, as always. He's my younger brother and he's a superstar in the VJ booth. Pushing my way through everyone, as no one moves out of my way, I head straight to the toilets.

I hear them before I see them. Two guys are punching the shit out of each other in front of the ladies' toilets. "What the fuck is going on here?" I shout. They both turn to face me and realise very quickly that I mean business. Hunter has followed me through to the hallway and as I grab one of the lads, Hunter grabs the other and we push them up against the wall.

"He was hitting on my girlfriend!" one of them says.

"I fucking wasn't. She was hitting on me."

"I don't give a flying fuck who was hitting on who. Which girl is she?" I ask, not so politely.

They both point at one of the girls who was crying and screaming. I look her up and down.

"Lads, no girl is worth fighting over. Just get a drink and forget about her."

The girl starts to get lippy with me for calling her out. "Are you going to let him talk about me like that?" she says to the guy I have against the wall.

"He hasn't got a choice, girl." I lean forward and talk

into his ear. "I'm going to give you the benefit of the doubt, 'cos I'm feeling generous tonight, but if I see you coming within two feet of this guy here, then I'm going to personally pick you up and throw you out. Do you hear me?"

The guy nods.

"Do you HEAR me?" I shout in his ear.

"Yes." He grunts. I let him go and he grabs his girl-friend's hand and drags her through to the bar.

I walk up to Hunter and repeat the same thing in the other guy's ear.

Hunter lets him go and he goes back out to the bar.

Hunter taps me on the shoulder. "Thanks, Zac. How you doing tonight?"

"Not bad. It's a busy one." I know he's not talking about Mixology, but I don't want to talk about it. Not now and not ever.

"Like that, huh? Okay, I'd better get back to the bar. See you later." I walk down the corridor and out the back for some fresh air.

I really want to punch someone. I want someone to start a fight with me so I can get some of this aggression out of me. I hate feeling this tightly strung. I punch the wall and shout "*Argh!*" into the air. It makes me feel a little bit better but it's not enough to calm me down.

Making my way back out to Ainsley, I see a group of girls waiting in line to get in. One of them is quite cute. I shake my head. I'm not interested in cute. Cute is not a good look for me. "All sorted out," I say to Ainsley.

She smiles at me and then nods in the direction of the queue. "We've got some lively ones out there."

"I see that. You aren't letting that group of girls in, are you? They're wasted."

"Come on, Zac. They're good-looking and will have

lots of fun. That's what we want our punters to have. Fun!" She's annoyed because I want to spoil the party for the group of girls. The only reason I want to do that is because they have drunk enough and don't really need to drink anymore. Any more drink and they could get themselves into serious trouble. I don't want that hanging over my head.

I can't stop watching them though. Especially the cute one. She is petite and hardly wearing anything. They're all laughing, but when I look past that, they're all swaying in the queue and practicing looking sober. If I wasn't so annoyed, I'd be laughing at them.

When they're at the front of the queue Ainsley opens the door for them. "Ains, what are you doing?" I grind out.

"I'm letting the customers in." She stares at me.

I moan internally; I just know they're going to be trouble.

As the girls walk through the front door, the cute one trips. I reach out and grab her before she falls.

"What are you doing, arsehole?" she shouts, stepping out of my arms. "Get your hands off me." She turns round to Ainsley. "You need to control your staff; they can't be manhandling the customers like that."

My whole body stiffens as I try to stop myself from exploding. Ainsley turns to look at me and shrugs her shoulders. She whispers, "Take a deep breath and open the door for them."

I shake my head. She stares at me. She knows there is going to be trouble.

"Sorry, girls. You're not getting in tonight," I say, standing in front of the door leading in to the bar.

"What the fuck do you mean we're not getting in? Is that because I didn't want you touching me, Zac James?"

It stuns me that she knows my name, but only for a minute.

"No, the reason I'm not letting you in is that you are all drunk enough and don't need any more. That's why I'm not letting you in, princess."

She squares up to me. "I'm not your princess and you are far from my prince."

I have to look down at her; she barely reaches my shoulders. Smiling, I realise I enjoy riling her. She is biting at everything I say.

"You're all drunk and not coming into my bar," I say, looking into her eyes.

She starts laughing and steps closer. "Ha! It's not your bar. It belongs to your brother and you're just the hired help!" She jabs her finger into my chest with each word.

One of her friends lunges at her. "Issy, stop! Let's just go." She tries to pull her away from me.

Issy shrugs her off. "Fuck off, Katelynn. I'm talking to HIM!" She pokes me once again.

I look over to Ainsley and she's shaking her head. She knows I won't be able to leave it alone.

"Okay, ladies, the fun is over. Come back another night and if you aren't so drunk, then you can come in." I turn to open the door for them to go back outside when Issy reaches out to open the door I moved away from.

I might be a big guy, but I have quick reflexes. Turning, I grab a hold of Issy and pick her up.

"Zac, put her down!" Ainsley says, trying to grab my arm to put Issy back on the floor.

"You are NOT going in there, princess. You are too drunk."

"I'm not drunk," she says, slurring.

"If you weren't drunk, I wouldn't have been able to pick you off the floor and pin you to the wall."

I can't hear anyone except her. She stares at me and I notice that she looks to the floor and then back at me. "Put me down, you fucker."

"You are falling all over the place. You need to go home."

"I remember seeing you falling all over the place, Zac James." She spits my name out. "Thinking you were superior to everyone else, and there you were, drinking and fighting yourself into oblivion."

I drop her and take a step back. My old life is totally separate to my life now. I did some bad things and don't like to be reminded of it.

"What the fuck do you know?" I growl at her.

She steps towards me again. "I know who you are. I know what you're capable of and I know you were a drunk waste of space not so long ago."

I reach out to grab her again, but suddenly I'm pulled backwards by both arms.

"Fuck off and leave me alone!" I shout at whoever is behind me.

"You need to calm down, brother," Hunter says, pulling me out of the front door and down the street.

Keaton has my other arm and the two of them are sweating, trying to drag me.

I shrug out of their hold and sit on a chair outside the Seaview Café.

"What the fuck were you doing, Zac? She's a girl. What is wrong with you?"

"She was rubbing me up the wrong way. She was pushing me, Hunter."

"She's a fucking girl."

I shake my head. "I know! I'm sorry!"

They both sit down next to me. "Zac, you've been

doing so well. I know today is a hard day for you. I think you should go home. Keaton can look after the door."

I think about what could have happened. I wouldn't have hit her. I just wanted to prove a point.

"Fuck you." I stand up. "I can do this. It won't affect me again." I walk towards Mixology and look around. I can't see the group of girls anymore, so I stand at the door with Ainsley and watch the rest of the queue coming in.

THERE'S NO MORE TROUBLE, thank God, and it's soon time to start moving people out. As soon as I open the door to the bar, I see her. Ainsley must have let them in when Hunter and Keaton took me next door. She has been backed into a corner by two guys. I make my way closer to them. Watching. Waiting.

Her friends are trying to get to her to leave, but the two guys aren't moving. Her eyes are looking around, trying to find her way out. They land on mine, and for a second, I see her weighing up which situation is the better one. Me or the two guys. She's lucky because she picks the better option. Me.

She looks at me with fear in her eyes. I recognise that look. I point at myself and then to her and she nods.

I don't hesitate any longer. I stomp over to the two guys. Lo and behold. it's the two guys from earlier. "Well. look who we have here. Did you two stop fighting? You took my advice and ditched the ugly girlfriend. That's great. But my advice is, stay away from this one; she has a hell of a punch."

One of the guys turns to me and says, "Why are you in our faces again? We're not fighting."

"Really? You want me to tell you why I'm about to

throw your asses out on the street? What are you doing to this girl? Huh?"

"She wants both of us. She was dancing with us," the other guy says.

"Sorry, does she look like she's enjoying this?" I say, looking at Issy. She is petrified. I'm angry at these two guys for putting her in this position, but I'm grateful too, because it proves my point from earlier.

"Excuse me, Issy, are you okay? Are you able to handle yourself or do you need me to remove these gentlemen?" I ask sarcastically.

"Fuck you, Zac," she says, not moving from her position. "Get them the fuck away from me."

She doesn't need to repeat herself. I lunge forward and grab the two guys by their shoulders and dig my fingers into their collarbones.

"Ow, fuck off," one guy says, trying to get away from my grip.

I march them away from the girls and out the front door. "Get out and stay out. You're both barred. Ainsley, get a good look at their faces, because they aren't welcome here anymore." I slam the door after throwing them onto the street. They give me the finger and walk off.

"Making friends with the customers again?" Ainsley says, smiling.

I ignore her and walk back inside to find Issy and her friends. They're hugging Issy and I see she's crying. I go over to them.

"Are you okay?" I ask her.

She nods her head, but doesn't say a word. That in itself speaks a thousand words to me.

I touch her on her shoulder and when she turns to face me, I pull her into a hug. I don't know what's come over me. "Listen, you'll be okay. Just try not to get so drunk the next time you go out. Bad things can happen when you're not in control of yourself, princess."

Her body stiffens. "I'm not your princess," she says and pulls away.

I chuckle. "Whatever. It's time for you ladies to leave. We're closing and you need to go home to your beds."

They turn and walk out, saying goodbye to Ainsley on their way.

HUNTER LOCKS the door as we all stand outside Mixology. "Right, another great night. See you all at Mum's for dinner tomorrow."

"Night," I say and turn to walk away.

"Zac. Do you want to go somewhere for a late drink?" Hunter asks.

"No, thanks. I'm going home. Sorry about earlier."

"As long as you're okay, that's all that matters."

"I'm fine!" I stomp off down the road.

It's beautiful walking along the seafront, but I don't even look at it anymore. I hate this town. I always have. I left here as soon as I could and moved to London. I got a great job in the city as a market trader and lived the high life. But it all turned to shit and I ended up back here.

Grabbing my bag out of my car, I turn up from the harbour, up one of the side streets. It gets dark as there are no street lights. I turn down another alley and there is nothing along here except a large warehouse. Walking past it, I hear some noises. Shit. I stop. I know I should keep walking. I know I should ignore the noises. But I fucking can't. I know what those noises are and I know what they do to me. I look behind me, take a deep breath, and walk up to the warehouse door. I knock sharply three times, then four times, then once. The lookout on the door slides it open and I see two big eyes looking back at me.

"Fuck, Zac. Haven't seen you for a while." The door opens further and I slip inside.

Benny, the guy who works the door, gives me a man hug.

"How long is it?"

"A year." I say, not offering any more information.

"Well, that's a year too long." He walks with me to the bar.

There's music playing. There's a lot of smoke swirling around the room, making the visibility poor. I guess the smoking ban hasn't made it in here yet. There's a *thump thump* noise which sounds like it's in time to the beat of the music. There's girls with hardly any clothes on everywhere and it makes me think, briefly, of Issy.

I smile to myself. She was a little rocket. She gave me as good as she got. She was tiny, but deadly. I pity the poor fucker who ends up with her. Although, tonight was the first time I had any feelings at all. She stirred something in me and I'm not sure I like it.

"I'll have a bottle of beer and a Rémy please." I turn to face away from the bar to look around and see who's here. The same old faces and a few new ones.

When my drinks are ready, I throw a tenner over the bar and pick them up, walking over to the centre of the room. I lean against a pillar to watch what's going on.

In the middle of the room is a boxing ring and there are two goons fighting each other. There is a lot of shouting. A lot of betting. A lot of smoking and a lot of scantily clad girls. Yeah, this feels like home.

I know I can only come here tonight. Tonight, I have an excuse. If I allow myself to come here more than once a year, I will slip back into my old ways.

I walk over to Ted; he's the promoter for the night. "Hey, Ted. What's going on tonight?"

He nods in the direction of the ring. "New guy up there. He's beaten five of our best guys in the last couple of months." He looks up at me. "You want to fight tonight? I was expecting you in. I thought you might be in earlier."

"Had a lot going on at the bar. Yeah, you know I want to fight. That's what I'm here for, not the exciting conversation, arsehole."

He laughs. "Still polite and eloquent, I see." He looks down at his book and rifles through it. "I could have a spot in an hour. You game?"

"You know it!" I smile and shake his hand.

"You want to know who you're fighting?"

"Nah, I don't care. I just need to pummel the shit out of someone tonight; I don't need to know their name." Smiling, I turn on my heel and sit down and watch the rest of the fight.

AFTER I CHANGE, I walk back into the room and everyone stops me to talk to me. That's what happens when you only come once a year. Everyone wants to talk and everyone wants to know when I'm coming back regularly again. I tell them all the same thing. "I'm not!"

Ted calls me over and tells me I will be fighting a relative newcomer. I hold up my hand to stop him telling me his name. Ted chuckles. "You've got ten minutes, then you're on, kiddo."

I watch the fight that's just wrapping up and I swear I see something out of the corner of my eye that attracts my attention. When I turn to look, there's nothing there. Strange. I hear something familiar too, but when I turn around, I don't hear it again. I must be hallucinating because of what day it is.

Ted nods for me to get warmed up and by the ring. He jumps into the ring and then grabs the mic. "Ladies and gentlemen, we have a treat in store for you all this evening. A long-time friend of ours is back for one night only. Please put your hands together and welcome back to The Underground... Zac James." Everyone starts clapping, wolf whistling, and calling my name. I miss this.

I jump into the ring and take one of the corners.

Ted continues. "We have a newcomer in our midst who is going to have to step up his game if he wants to win against one of our old favourites. Please welcome Micky O'Shay." The crowd claps, but only half-heartedly.

I'm in the corner when I watch Micky climb into the ring. Walking over to him, I shake his hand, like the true gentleman I am.

IT'S the third round and I'm only getting started. Unfortunately, Micky is having a few problems. He has some cuts and bruises on his face. He seems to be losing his balance and, to be honest, I've had my fun. I move closer to him, and with one last punch up towards his chin, he falls to the floor and doesn't get back up again. The crowd goes wild and I can feel the adrenaline coursing through me.

"And the winner is... Zac James," Ted says, holding my hand in the air. I look around at everyone getting pleasure from our fight and I'm sure I see Issy. What the fuck is she doing here?

As soon as Ted drops my hand, I jump out of the ring and make my way to the bar. There's a bottle of beer and a Rémy waiting for me. I drink the Rémy down straight then take the bottle of beer with me to the changing room.

ZAC

After a quick shower, I get dressed and make my way back out to the bar. I don't normally stay after a fight, I usually slink away back to my normal life. Tonight though, I want to stay. I need to see if Issy is here.

There's another fight about to start, and I hear Ted announcing the fighters. "In the blue corner is the reigning, undefeated, champion of The Underground... Sweeney Todd." I smile to myself. He is only undefeated because he hasn't fought me. I'm not a regular, unless you call once a year regular, so I don't get to fight the main guys.

As Sweeney Todd starts to climb into the ring, I see Issy hugging him. Fuck. That puts a new perspective on everything. But then I see him kiss one of her friends. It's a long and passionate kiss, and when I watch Issy, she doesn't seem to be jealous. What the hell is going on?

I watch her for a short while as she watches the fight. Eventually, she comes over to the bar and spots me sitting at the end. She struts over to me. "Didn't think I'd see you in here. Guess your family don't know everything about you then."

"You were supposed to go home, Issy. Why are you still drinking?" I ask, taking a sip of my beer.

"None of your business."

Just then, the barman comes over to serve her. "Hey, Issy. How's things?"

"Great, except I see you've lowered the standards here tonight." She nods towards me.

I growl and move closer to her. The barman knows me well and shrugs. I'm right next to her and I say in her ear, "You're pushing my buttons, princess."

"Really?" She turns towards me with her hands on her hips. She is gorgeous and my body starts reacting to her. What the fuck? She leans in. "I remember seeing you here years ago, Zac James. You were a drunk and a great fighter. You can't tell me what to do. Is it '*do as I say, not as I do*?'"

I have the urge to lean in and kiss her just to stop her talking. She is hitting me where it hurts and she doesn't even realise it.

"I have my own reasons for being here, princess. What are yours? What are you doing hanging off Sweeney Todd, anyway? Didn't pin you as a fighting slut."

I hear her hand coming through the air before it hits me on the face. I don't move. I deserved that. I know I did.

"Don't you dare call me a slut, pretty boy. I am the furthest from a slut you will ever find."

What does she mean by that? "Listen, if you're hanging around him, then that's just what you are. I'm leaving, but you'd better think twice before coming in my bar again. I don't like throwing the trash out two nights in a row!"

She opens her mouth to say something back to me, but she can't. She doesn't know what to say. I smile to myself. I down my beer, pick up my bag, and walk out of The Underground to make my way home.

WALK OF SHAME

2 OZ VODKA, 1 OZ BLACKBERRY SYRUP, ¾ OZ LIME JUICE,
FRESH BLACKBERRIES, FRESH RASPBERRIES, GINGER ALE OR
CHAMPAGNE, TO TOP

FIVE YEARS AGO
Mum and Dad were up within a few hours of my phone call, and when they walked into the hospital room, I broke down again. Everything happened in a blur. Not long after they came, Erika's parents came and sat with us. The doctor finally came in and said, "I'm sorry. She had huge internal bleeding and some of her major organs were crushed beyond repair."

I stood up. "What do you mean beyond repair?"

"I'm sorry. We couldn't save her."

I didn't listen to anymore. I stood up and started kicking the chairs and punching the wall. My dad got up and pulled me away from the wall and tried to calm me down. He hugged me and wouldn't let go until I stopped sobbing. I'll be honest, I don't really know what happened over the next few months. Mum and Dad didn't go home for at least two months and that was only because I told them to fuck off and leave me alone. I know there was a funeral and I vaguely remember turning up, giving a speech and then getting absolutely paralytic.

I drank, fought, and fucked my way through the next two years, oblivious to the carnage I was leaving behind. I didn't speak to my family for ten months and that was when they intervened.

THREE YEARS AGO

"Stop knocking at the fucking door leave me alone!" I shout. My friends know not to knock. The knocking keeps going. Fuck's sake, now I'm going to have to get up and open the door.

I swing the door open and am barged by four people. Two big men, a woman, and a smaller guy push me back into the house and slam the doors. "Sit in the fucking chair and listen to us," Hunter says as he and Keaton almost throw me into the chair.

"Fuck off. I don't need you," I say, not really meaning it.

When I look up, Hunter, Keaton, Ainsley, and Skylar are standing in front of me with their arms folded. I can see disappointment in their eyes. That hurts more than anything they're about to say.

"You're coming home with us, Zac. We can't watch you throw your life away anymore. We've given you two years to grieve and sort your life out," Hunter says.

"Zac, we love you, but we can't stand by and watch you kill yourself slowly. All this drinking, fighting and whatever the hell else you're doing is going to kill you and we won't let that happen," Ainsley says.

"Fuck you."

Skylar sits next to me; he's the youngest in our family. I don't really know him that well as I moved out years ago. "Zac, I look up to you, I always have. I don't want you grieving any longer. It's tearing our family apart. Mum isn't the same. She's lost her spark and it's your fault. You need to come home and fix that shit!"

I can feel tears in my eyes. I never want to hurt my mum; she means too much to me. She's always there for me, even when I push her away.

Ainsley sits down in front of me and takes my hands. "Zac, come home. We want to take care of you. We want our brother back."

I cry. I actually cry. My brothers and sister want me to come home. I hadn't even noticed Keaton wasn't in the room when he came bounding down the stairs with a suitcase. "Right, I'm packed. Let's get him home!" he says as he walks towards the front door.

"Come on, Zac. Let's go," Hunter says as they all stand. They aren't letting me say no. Then again, they know I don't really want to say no. I need rescuing. I need my family.

NO ONE TALKS during the five hour journey. When we pull up at Mum and Dad's, I start to feel nervous. My heart starts racing and my head hurts. I'm not looking forward to facing them. I just hope Mum doesn't see through my pain. I've caused them heartache and pain and that kills me. I need to man up and get my act together.

Hunter turns off the engine. "Right, Mum has Sunday dinner on the go. She's not expecting you. She doesn't know that we had to go and intervene and bring you home. You need to go in first and make peace with Mum. We'll follow you in a short while."

"Thanks, Hunter. Thanks, guys." I climb out of his car and make my way to the front door. I knock and then open it. "Hi, I'm home."

"Kitchen," Dad says.

Taking a deep breath, I walk into the kitchen. I lean against the door jamb, like I always did.

Mum turns around. She smiles and comes over to me. "Hey, Zac. What a surprise. Just in time for dinner. How long are you staying?"

"Erm, I'm moving home. I need to be close to my family."

"Welcome home, son," Dad says, handing me a drink. I take it, but don't drink it. I need to stay sober for a while.

The others come in and act surprised to see me. They don't want Mum and Dad to know what a mess I was.

Sunday dinner is much the same as it always has been. I realise how much I missed this by staying in London after Erika died.

"So, what are your plans, Zac?" Dad asks at the table.

"I'm not sure. It was kind of a spur of the moment decision to come home," I say, looking at Hunter and Keaton.

"Are you going to get a job?" Mum asks.

"I've made enough money not to work for a couple of years, so I want to see what's around and then make a decision. I'll start looking for a house as soon as I can, but can I stay here for a while?"

"Of course you can." Mum smiles at me.

"Great, that's settled then."

"You know you could come and work with us in Mixology. It's getting busier and we could use the help."

"I might do that. Give me a few months to get myself sorted and then let's talk again."

He nods at me. I am so lucky with my family. They really care about me.

THOSE WERE my famous last words. Six months later, I had moved into my own house and wallowed in my own self-pity. I had found The Underground through some friends of mine in London and I was fighting all day and night and then getting absolutely shitfaced after. I never missed Sunday dinner with the family though, and I was always sober on a Sunday. That's meant I was in control – didn't it?

Apparently not. I had had a huge fight the previous night with some guy and he had beaten me pretty bad. I knocked him out in the fourth round, but he did some damage to my ribs and it meant I couldn't go back for a while.

The Underground was slowly killing me. The fighting, drinking, and endless stream of unnamed women. I was spiralling out of control. I found out how much when Hunter and Keaton turned up at my doorstep, once again.

THEY BOTH COME into the house and stand there, looking around. There are beer cans all over the place. Pizza boxes, boxes of condoms, and lube just lying around on the dinner table. I remember that night; it was classy. I ate her out at the dinner table and then fucked her over it. Anyway, I digress.

"What the fuck are you doing, Zac?" Hunter shouts. "Do we have to fucking intervene again?"

"I didn't ask you to come here. You could just fuck off and leave me alone."

"Really?" Keaton says. "You mean that?"

"Yeah," I say, closing my eyes, just hoping they will go.

"While you're busy killing yourself, think about Erika. You are not the man she loved. That man has left the building and this arsehole has taken his place. Do you think she would want you to wallow like this? No, she fucking wouldn't."

I stand up. "What the fuck do you know about Erika? You don't have the right to bring her into this."

"No? I don't? I think I do. It's because of her that you're in this situation. Grow the fuck up and start putting your life back together. And if you don't want to do it for yourself, or even for Erika, then do it for Mum. She knows there's something going on with you. Even when you go for Sunday dinner, you're not really there."

"Leave me alone!"

"No," Hunter says. "Zac, we love you, you're our brother. But right now, we don't like you."

I slump back down on my chair. I love my brothers, even when they're being wankers, but the thought that they don't like me hurts me bad. I lean my head into my hands. I don't know what to say.

They both sit down and the tension leaves the room. "Zac, we want to help you," Keaton says.

"So we have a proposition for you," Hunter adds.

"What?" I mumble.

"You work out a lot and you're strong. We want you to come and work at Mixology. We're busy enough now that we need someone to stand on the door and get rid of people if they cause any trouble. You're the man for the job."

"Like a bouncer?" I ask.

"Look at it more like security," Hunter says, smiling. "What do you think? Join the family business, Zac."

"I don't know. I don't need to work."

"I'm happy not to pay you if that's what you want." Hunter laughs.

"We know you don't need to work, but we both think that you *need* to work," Keaton says.

"I erm… I don't know what to say. Why do you bother to keep coming to my rescue?"

"You're our brother and we know you're not really an arsehole," Hunter says, laughing.

"Fuck off." I laugh back at him. "What do I need to do to do this job then?"

"Well, the first thing you need to do is clear up this fucking house. It's like a disaster zone. I'm sure Ainsley will come over and help, and Sky too. What do you say?"

I groan. "Okay. Give me a couple of days to get my head together and then I'll start work."

"Right, that's good, because Ains and Sky are outside waiting with buckets and mops and bin bags." Keaton smiles. He goes over to the front door, opens it, whistles and waves them in.

I guess they weren't going to take no for an answer.

We spend the rest of the day and well into the night tidying and cleaning my house. It really was a shit tip. When they leave, after we've had a takeaway, I smile, knowing I've got the best family in the world.

LEATHER AND LACE

2oz GIN, ¾ OZ LEMON JUICE, ½ OZ SIMPLE SYRUP, ½ OZ CREME DE VIOLETTE, DASH OF GRENADINE, CHAMPAGNE TO TOP

PRESENT DAY
I wake up the day after my fight with Micky Flynn and thank God all my bruises are on my torso and not my face. I don't want to have to explain that to the family. Not after everything they did to bring me home. Anyway, I only go to The Underground once a year now, on Erika's anniversary. I don't like to be happy on that day. I don't deserve to be happy.

Getting out of bed, I think about Issy. During the first couple of years after Erika died, I slept with anything that offered itself, and when I was fighting, there were lots of offers. None of them meant anything. None of them even knew me. None of them interested me. I haven't been interested in anyone since I came home three years ago. So, why does Issy interest me?

I think it's because she fought back. She doesn't just bow down because she's scared of me or because she fancies me. No, she is a little fire rocket and a fighter. I like that about her. She's cute to look at too. Smiling, I walk into the bathroom and get in the shower. As the hot water cascades over me, I rub my hard cock. Morning glory and all that. However, this morning, it's different. Today is the first day I wank and don't think of Erika. I think about Issy when she slapped me and how it turned me on that she stood up to me. I lean one hand on the shower wall as I pull my cock with the other hand, gripping it tight while I pump it. It doesn't take long before I can feel the old feelings coming up through my body and I release all over the wall. For the first time in a very long time, I don't feel satisfied. I need a real woman to satisfy me and I'm going to find me one.

I head to the gym after breakfast and do some training. I need to stay in shape for Mixology and you never know when you need a bit of muscle.

I meet the family at Mixology in the afternoon to help with some of the orders. I do the heavy carrying and everyone else puts it all away. That's just the way we work. Before we leave, Hunter calls me to his office.

"What's up?" I ask.

"I just wanted to make sure you're okay. You know, after last night."

"I'm good. I'm sorry about the way I acted. I shouldn't have done it. She just tipped me over the edge, and because of the day it was, I just lost it. But I'm sorted now. I'm calm."

"I hope so, Zac. If you repeat that, we're going to have a more serious chat."

I roll my eyes. Hunter is a great guy, but he loves lording it over us others.

"No problem, boss. Message received," I say before I walk out the door and through the bar.

"See you all tonight," I say, walking to the front door. I need to clear my head.

The seafront is the best place to clear your mind. The sea is crashing against the rocks, the salt in the air sticks to your skin, and if you close your eyes, all you can hear is the sound of the seagulls. You could be anywhere in the world. A lot of the time when I walk along the seafront and close my eyes, I think of Erika. My sweet, beautiful, Erika and where we would be now. The kids we would have, the family we would have become. It's torture to think about her, because I know I can't have those things with her anymore.

Today, of course, I think of Issy. What is it about this girl that has crawled under my skin? I haven't been with another woman since my brothers came and cleaned me up. Now, I need to find a woman who will scratch the itch I have. That will get Issy out of my head.

THREE HOURS LATER, after I've showered and got ready for work, I walk in the door of Mixology. Keaton has my cup of coffee ready for me and I stand at my post just inside the door with Ainsley.

"Hey, Ains. How's things with you today?"

"Not too bad. Hope it's not busy tonight. I'm tired and need to get home to my bed."

"Alone, I hope," I say, laughing. Ainsley gets a really hard time from us boys. If any guy tries it on with her, we always push them away. She's our sister and we don't want guys touching her. If she wants to start a relationship, she's going to have to move it away from Mixology.

"For God's sake. Why can't I have a relationship? You guys piss me off."

I chuckle because she is so easy to wind up.

"We just want you to make sure you end up with the right guy. We don't want you to go through hell to get there. We've all been through some shit and don't want that happening to you too."

"I know and I appreciate it, I really do. But please just let me find out these things by myself."

Even when she goes into some of the other bars, she's being watched by our friends who either report back to us or interrupt her to ask how she is. She gets really pissed off and storms back here. We love it though.

We open the doors and Ainsley's best friend, Callie, comes through first. "Hey, Ains," she says, hugging her and kissing her on the cheeks. She then turns to face me. "Hey, big boy, haven't seen you in a while." She hugs me and kisses me too.

"Hey, Callie. What's been keeping you away?"

"Relationship drama. You know what girls are like. They get so clingy and need you to explain everything."

I laugh. Callie is a lesbian and the stories she tells us are hilarious.

"We need to catch up soon," I say to her.

"Too right." She turns to look at Ainsley. "See you later, sweets." She heads into the bar.

I look at Ainsley and she's blushing. I wonder if she fancies Callie. *No way!*

The crowds flood in o Mixology and it looks like it's going to be another busy night. Just as I start relaxing, I catch something red out of the corner of my eye. When I turn, I'm face to face with Issy. What the fuck? I told her not to come back here.

"Hey, Isabella," Ainsley says. "No trouble tonight, I hope."

Issy is still looking at me and says, "Not on my part. Can't say much for pretty boy here."

I stare at her. "I told you you weren't welcome here again."

"Zac, what did you do that for?"

Still staring at Issy, but talking to Ainsley, I say, "This girl is trouble with a capital T. I told her I don't like to throw the trash out two nights on the trot."

"Zac James! Where are your manners? How dare you? She is a customer, she isn't drunk, and she wants to spend money in our bar. She's going in."

Issy smiles up at me. "Looks like you're going to have to let me in, pretty boy." She starts laughing and then walks into the bar. I punch the wall.

"For fuck's sake, Ains. She is trouble, I'm telling you."

"Zac, calm down. If you fancy her just go and ask her out. I think she likes you because she keeps calling you pretty boy."

"I do not fancy her. I do not like her. When she causes trouble, don't come asking me to sort it all out."

Ainsley just shakes her head at me and then lets some more people in. This time it's a group of guys who are a little worse for wear.

"Guys, before you go in there, I'm warning you. Any trouble and you're out. Do you hear me?"

"Yeah, no worries," one of them says before heading into the bar.

There's a steady stream of customers tonight and no trouble, thank God. It's eleven o'clock, which means it's my break. "I'm going for a coffee, Ainsley. Do you want one too?" I ask as I have the door open to the bar.

"Yeah. Thanks, Zac."

Walking into the bar, I take a minute to look over it. Mixology has been really successful and it's all down to our family. We all work hard in our respective places. I didn't want to work here when I first came home. They were having a hard time keeping me out of the pubs, clubs, and the Underground. But as I realised I was on a path of self-destruction, I knew I needed to sort myself out.

I spot Issy dancing. She's not hard to spot in her red dress that clings to every curve she has, and by God, is she curvy. She has the typical hourglass figure, but she isn't skinny. I can't stop staring at her as she gyrates on the dance floor. She turns as if she knew I was thinking about her and she smiles at me and moves her hips even faster.

Just then, the group of guys join the girls on the dance floor and one of them gets behind Issy and dances in time to her movements. It looks like she's gyrating against his cock. I'm mesmerized and can't look away. He grabs her waist and pulls her back into his body and she continues gyrating as she stares at me. She smiles at me and then throws her head back as if she's really enjoying the sensation of this guy mauling her. I have to walk away; I can't watch her any longer so I make my way to the kitchen to make some coffee.

Leaning against the wall, waiting for the kettle to boil, I hear a small knock on the door. When I open it, Issy pushes her way inside.

"Why were you staring at me dancing?" she asks, with her hands on my chest, trying to push me against the wall. "Did you enjoy watching me move my hips like that? Were you thinking about what I could do to you in bed?"

What the fuck? She must be pissed.

"Look, Issy, I don't fuck drunk girls. I don't take sloppy seconds either. So, if you're going to let that guy molest you then good luck. I hope you enjoy it. He isn't going to be any good though because he's had too much to drink. That will make him selfish. He will only think about his own release, not yours. If that's what you want, then knock yourself out."

She puts her hands on my chest again and I feel something strange. I realise I want her to run her hands down my chest.

"Don't forget, I know you, Zac. I know you fuck drunk girls. They were the only ones you could get at one time. But you wouldn't fuck me. So, if anyone would be getting sloppy seconds around here then it would be me." She looks up into my eyes and I see a fire in them that I hadn't noticed before. She looks down at my mouth and it's at that moment I realise I want to kiss her.

I wrap my hands around her waist and pull her in close. "I used to fuck drunk girls. Now I'm a lot more fussy." Her hands are still on my chest and I'm sure she can feel how aroused I am having her this close.

I put my hand around to the back of her neck and tilt her head so all I have to do is lean down and kiss those plump lips that are slightly open, waiting for my tongue to invade them.

Suddenly, the door opens. "Where is Ainsley's cup of cof …." Keaton stops talking as he sees us. Issy steps away and runs out of the door.

"What the fuck, Keaton?"

He chuckles. "Sorry, mate. I was only looking for Ainsley's coffee. She said you had been gone for ages. Now I know why. Sorry if I interrupted you." He turns and walks out again.

"Fuck!" I shout into the room. I make two cups of coffee and walk back out through the bar and see Issy dancing again. Why does she look even more beautiful this time around? I watch as the guy puts his arm around her again and pulls her back into him. She looks at me and smiles, so I do what anyone else would do. I turn away and walk back out to the front door.

"What the hell took you so long?" Ainsley asks, taking her cup of coffee.

"I got caught up," I say, drinking mine.

We get some more customers, and every time I open the door to let them in, I see Issy dancing and staring at me.

"Zac, we need you in here." Keaton's voice comes through my earpiece.

"Got to go, Ains," I say, handing her my cup.

As soon as I open the door to the bar, I see a commotion on the dancefloor. There is a guy on the floor and a group of people standing around him. There is a lot of shouting as I run up to the group.

The guy that was dancing with Issy is on the floor. She's sat on top of him, punching him. I want to laugh. The size of him and he's being beaten up by a girl half his size. But I have to stay professional.

I wade into the middle of the circle. "What the fuck's going on here?" I say, reaching out to pull Issy off the guy. She shrugs me off.

"He started molesting me." She stands in front of me with her hands on her hips.

"Well, from what I saw earlier, you didn't mind it."

I reach down and help the guy up. "Thanks, mate." He tries to walk away, but I grab his arm. "I'm not finished with you yet. I told you and your friends earlier, any trouble and you'd be out."

"I didn't start this, she did!" He points at Issy.

"No, I didn't," she says, flying at him again. I manage to grab her and pull her back so she has her back against my chest.

"Don't you move. I'm dealing with you next," I growl into her ear.

"Fuck you."

I ignore her and look at the guy. "Get your friends and get out of here. I don't want any more trouble from you. If you don't get out then I'll have to remove you myself."

The guy just stands there.

"Do you hear me?" I shout. He starts to turn to his friends and I watch them leave through the front door.

"Right, everyone, back to what you were doing. Nothing more to see," I say, taking Issy's hand and pulling her through the bar and out of the back door. The door slams behind us.

"What the fuck was that about, Issy?"

"That guy was touching me and I didn't want him to touch me!" she shouts. She's pacing up and down.

"I saw you dancing with him earlier and you didn't mind him touching you. Sending mixed messages to a guy can get you in a lot of trouble."

"He had no right to touch me, even though I was dancing with him. Guys think they have the right, but they don't."

"Listen, if you gyrate on a guy like you were, then he is going to assume you want to fuck him!"

She turns to look at me. "No way. I didn't want that at all." She looks sorry for herself.

"What did you want then?"

She looks at me. "I wanted to make you angry!"

"So, you dirty dance with a stranger to make me angry? Why the fuck would you do that? You hate me. All you have to do is shout at me and it makes me angry."

"I don't hate you." She looks at the floor.

"Yes, you do."

"No, I don't." She looks up at me.

All of a sudden I hear, "Zac, get here now," in my ear.

"I have to go. Just keep away from the guys that you don't want and don't let them touch you," I say, grabbing her hand and pulling her back inside. As soon as we're in the door, I let go and rush into the bar. The guys who were dancing with Issy and their friends are back and they don't look happy.

I see them look past me and the guy starts moving towards Issy. What the fuck does he think he's doing?

I grab his arm as he goes to walk past me. "What the fuck did I say to you? Get out of my bar and don't come back. That isn't the way out." He tries to pull out of my grip, but I grip him tighter.

"She's a fucking slut. She's a tease. It's her that should be made to leave," he says, hurling abuse about Issy.

"You don't get to talk about her that way." I start pulling him out of the bar; I need to move this outside.

Unfortunately, Issy is following us. He is spitting insults at her and she's spitting them back to him. This is going to get ugly quickly.

"Issy, go back inside. Let me deal with this lowlife," I say, turning to face her.

"No! I won't let him call me names like that."

When we're outside, the guy tries to take a swing at me. Issy screams and jumps on him. What the fuck is she doing?

I pull her off him. "Stay there," I say and turn to the guy, pushing him against the wall. "Fuck off before I call the police. Don't come back," I say, watching him and his friends walking down the street, giving me the middle finger as they go.

"Don't come back, you fuckers!" Issy shouts. She looks like she wants to go after them and fight them. I chuckle to myself then I grab her and drag her around the corner.

"What the fuck were you doing? I told you to stay in the bar. Why did you come out here and jump on him?"

"He was going to hurt you. Anyway, he was a fucker,"

she says, totally serious.

I look in her eyes, taking a deep breath, I can't help myself. I lift her up so she's eye level with me and push her against the wall.

"You drive me crazy, Issy," I say, before crushing my lips to hers. She doesn't even hesitate. She opens them immediately and our tongues fight for power.

She wraps her legs around my waist and her hands around my neck and we continue kissing for about ten minutes. When I eventually pull away, she moans.

"Why did you stop? I was enjoying that."

I laugh. "I have work to do and you've been stopping me from doing my job for the last two nights."

I try to unravel her from me, but she won't get down.

"Issy, I have to go." I grab hold of her legs and untie them. She still clings onto my neck as I slowly slide her down my body.

"You are such a spoilsport, you know? I was just starting to have some fun with you."

"I have to go." I turn and walk back inside. I don't know why I kissed her. For the first time in years, I feel guilty for kissing another woman.

THE REST of the night is quiet. I've had enough trouble for tonight. Except, of course, it doesn't work out that way. When we're getting the customers out at the end of the night, there is one waiting for me. Issy.

What the fuck is she waiting for? The kiss was a mistake. I can't let it happen again. She infuriates me.

"What are you waiting for, Issy? We're locking up. You need to go home."

"I thought you might want to go to The Underground with me when you finish."

I look around to make sure no one overheard her. "I only go there once a year."

"Why?"

"Why what?"

"Why do you only go once a year? You could make some really good money, you know? Sweeney makes a fortune."

"Oh, yeah. I forgot you were one of his sluts," I say before I even realise it.

"Fuck you," she says as she goes to slap me – again.

I grab her hand this time and pull her close to me. "Stop trying to slap me."

"Stop calling me a slut!" She grits her teeth, staring at me. We come together and kiss again. This time it's extremely heated and she has her legs wrapped around me quicker than I can breathe. Her arms are curled tightly in my hair and she's pulling it wildly. God, she's like a drug and I can't wait for my next hit.

I push her against the window of the bar and I can't get enough of her. I grab her arse and pull it closer to me. She moans. "God, Zac, you annoy me so much, but I want you even more."

"You infuriate me, Issy." My lips crash down on hers again and there is no doubt as to how much I'm enjoying this. I'm harder than I have been in years.

"Take me home, Zac. Please?"

I moan and kiss her again. If I take her home then I'm going to break her, I just know it.

"Let's slow this down a little. We can go to The Underground and have a late drink and talk. All we've done is argue and kiss. Then we can decide what happens later."

I feel her body relax into mine. "Okay," she says and slides down my body. I grab her hand and shout into the rest of the family. "See you guys tomorrow. I'm off."

UNDERGROUND

1 TBSP AVERNA AMARO, 1 OZ RUM, 1 TBSP APEROL, 2 DASHES MOLE BITTERS, 3 DASHES ORANGE BITTERS, 3 OZ CHAMPAGNE

We haven't spoken since we left Mixology, but we walk along the seafront and soon find ourselves outside The Underground. Issy moves to do the secret knock on the door and I find myself wondering again why she comes here. I move in front of her. "I'm a gentleman." I chuckle. Knocking three times, then four times, then once, the shutter slides open and Benny lets us in.

"Two nights on the trot, Zac?" Benny says. "We don't see you for a year and then you can't stop coming back." He sees Issy and then looks down to our hands that are clasped together. "I thought you two had an argument last night."

"Yeah, we did. But he saw the error of his ways," Issy says, laughing.

I ignore them both and make my way to the bar to

order a bottle of beer and a Remy. Issy comes up behind me, and as soon as she touches me, I feel a spark throughout the whole of my body. I turn and run my hand along her waist and around her back to pull her close. Leaning forward, I go to kiss her, but she moves out of my grasp.

"Issy, what the *fuck* are you doing here tonight?" I hear and, turning around, I see Sweeney Todd walking up and hugging her.

"I wanted a couple of late night drinks, Damien. That's allowed, you know." She knows his first name. This isn't good. What have I got myself into?

Stepping away from the bar, I say, "Well, it was nice to see you again, Issy. I'll be off now." I don't wait for her to say anything, I just walk to the front door. This was a mistake. I don't need to be someone else's dirty secret. I don't need to get in the middle of two people.

Just as I get to the door, I hear my name.

"Zac, wait!"

Turning towards her, I don't give her a chance to speak. "This was a mistake, Issy. I shouldn't be here."

"Are you running away from me?"

"No, I'm running away from this lifestyle. I can't be here."

I walk out of the door and home, where I stand on my balcony. Yes, I have one too, and I shout into the wind. Issy is bad news. She was leading me into the lion's den, which I had promised I would never go into again. What was I thinking?

WAKING UP IN THE MORNING, I feel like I have a hangover, which is impossible because I left before I drank my beer. My mind is so confused with thoughts of Issy. I like her when I shouldn't. It's my fault Erika died and I shouldn't be allowed to find happiness with anyone else. She is somehow connected with The Underground and that is a place I can't go to and not slip back into my old ways. I am not that person any more.

Groaning, I roll over in bed. I don't feel like doing anything today. Turning on the TV, I watch endless trash and constantly flick from one programme to the next, shouting at the TV when the adverts are on every channel when I change it.

I sleep a lot today, and it's when I'm in one of these deep sleeps that my phone rings. I ignore it. I don't want to adult today.

It keeps ringing, and every time it goes to voicemail, it rings again. Shit, someone really needs to get hold of me.

I pick up the phone. "What do you want?" I don't even know who it is, but I have a feeling it's one of my siblings.

"Get your arse out of bed and get over here quick!" I was right; it's Hunter.

"Why should I? I don't want to do anything today."

"Zac, it's family dinner time and you're not here. Get over here now and Mum won't notice you're late." He hangs up.

Hunter knows I would do anything for Mum, especially after her coming to my rescue five years ago. I moan, get out of bed, shower, get changed and jump in my car and drive to my parents' house. Taking a deep breath, I knock on the door and walk in as they're carrying the dishes to the table. I pick up the last bowl and pop it on the table before I sit down. "Sorry, I'm late," I say to Mum and Dad, but I'm looking at Hunter.

"That's okay," Mum says, "You're here now."

Dinner is gorgeous as usual and then Mum asks us all

what has been happening since the last time we all sat down together.

"How have you been, Zac?" Mum asks. "I know it was five years the other day."

"I've been okay. Feeling a bit down today, but got over that quick enough," I say, looking straight at Hunter.

"You know you can come to me anytime," Mum says, smiling at me, and all I want to do is hug her. I clear my throat.

"I know, Mum. Maybe we can do lunch tomorrow or something." She smiles at me and nods.

"What's been happening with Mixology?" Dad asks.

"It's been busy these last few nights, which is great," Hunter says.

"What about the surfing, Keaton? How's that going?"

"Yeah, Dakota and I are training. We'll be leaving in a few weeks so we're doing as much as we can before we leave." Keaton looks at Dakota and holds her hand. I love watching my older brothers with their girlfriends. I never thought they would be soppy and fall in love and it amuses me.

"That's great, guys," Dad says. "Ainsley, what about you? Anything happening in your love life?"

She laughs. "No, and it doesn't help that any time a guy approaches me, one of my brothers runs him off."

I chuckle, as do my brothers.

"Good job, boys," Dad says.

"Skylar, what about you?"

"Not much going on. Still playing music." Skylar doesn't have much to say. He is definitely the quietest of us James'.

"So," Dad says. "I heard you've had a bit of trouble in the bar this week."

Shit. Where has he heard that from?

Hunter looks at me. "Yeah, Zac had to remove a couple of people from the bar and they got a bit rowdy. Nothing he couldn't handle though."

"Really? I heard you got handsy with a girl, Zac," Dad says.

Urgh. "She was being lippy. She was drunk and I was proving a point. I told her that she couldn't handle herself being drunk. I proved it by putting her in a compromising position before she even realised."

"But, she's a girl," he says, clearly disappointed.

"If you knew her you wouldn't say that."

"That's not what I would have said when I walked into the kitchen last night," Keaton says, laughing.

"Piss off, Keaton."

"Zac James, don't bring that language to our table," Mum says, and now I'm embarrassed as well as angry.

"I'm not hungry anymore. Don't expect me in tonight. At least then you know there'll be no more trouble." I stand and leave the table.

"Zac, come back here now," Mum says. I stop and turn to face her.

"Sorry, Mum. I can't. I need to go and be on my own for a while. Sorry."

Leaving the house, I jump in my car and drive around. I end up outside The Underground, and even though it's the middle of the day, I park the car and go inside. Benny is even more shocked to see me at this time of day than he was last night.

"Who pissed his bed today?" he asks, laughing at me.

"I need a drink." I walk up to the bar and order my usual.

It's only after I have drunk the beer and my Remy that I look around to see who's here.

There are a couple of young guys fighting in the ring

and the rest of the room is used for training. I feel like I need to fight some of this aggression out of me.

I call Benny over. "Hey, Benny. I need to train and then I want a fight."

"You've been out for a long time, Zac. Why do you want to start again?"

"I just need to do this. I've got a lot of suppressed anger and if I don't fight then I'm going to lose my family."

"I heard you've been fighting with Isabella."

"Isabella?" I think for a minute. "Oh, you mean Issy. Yeah. She drives me crazy. One minute I want to fight her and the next I want to kiss her."

"Yeah, I got that impression. She was kind of pissed last night that you left her here."

"She was with Sweeney, so I'm not playing anyone's third wheel." I signal for another drink.

"Sweeney Todd? As in Damien Sweeney? Oh my God, Zac. Damien is her brother."

"What? Her brother? I thought she was with him and trying to have me on the side." Now I feel an even bigger fool for pushing her away. This day is not going well at all.

Benny laughs loudly. "She got drunk last night and was very vocal about you. It was hilarious. She is going to die laughing when I tell her that you thought she was in a relationship with Damien."

I shake my head. I'm not going to live this down. "Actually, Benny, forget the training. I'm just drinking today."

Turning to face the bar, I say, "Keep the drinks coming as soon as you see them empty. I ain't moving from this chair all day." I'm going to drown my sorrows and nobody had better get in my way.

HOURS LATER, I can barely see in front of me. I haven't had much to drink over the last few years, so it affects me quite quickly. I feel pissed off, low, and alone.

My loneliness doesn't last long as the fighting sluts come in and they all try to talk to me. I'm not interested. I ignore them; I don't care how rude I'm being.

"So, you decided to come back then? You're only twelve hours too late. That ship sailed," I hear Issy say. She stands next to me. "What is your problem, Zac? What do you want from me?"

"I don't want anything from you. I don't want anything from anyone." I grab my beer and drink it down. As I bang it on the bar, another one is left for me.

"Drinking your woes away, are you? I've just been down to Mixology to see if you were there and your sister told me you didn't show. Hope there's no trouble down there tonight."

"Bitch! You're here, so there won't be any trouble down there tonight."

"Whatever your problem is, Zac, take it out on someone else." She turns to walk away and I can't help myself. I reach out and grab her arm. She stops and turns to face me.

"I don't want to be on my own tonight, Issy. Please?"

"You know something, Zac? You intrigue me. I know you want me and yet you push me away. Why is that? That's what I want to know. Is it worth putting up with your mood swings to find out? That's what I need you to prove to me." She turns to the barman. "Give me my usual please," she says as she pulls the chair up next to me.

"Issy, I'm complicated."

"I'd worked that out already." She laughs as she takes a sip of her drink. "You're lucky. I like complicated."

"Well, then you're hanging out with the right guy." We sit drinking for a while in silence.

She moves closer to me and reaches her hand out and puts it on my leg. It feels good. I put my hand on top of hers. She smiles at me and raises her drink. I raise mine and smile back at her.

We have fun, drinking and laughing for the next couple of hours, then the fighting starts. We watch the fights and then Sweeney Todd comes on. I laugh, thinking about how I thought they were a couple.

Issy looks at me and laughs. "Benny told me you thought me and Damien were together."

"Yeah, not one of my finer moments."

"Is that why you left last night?"

"Yeah. I told you. I don't want to be anyone's sloppy seconds."

She laughs and leans forward. "How about being my first?" she whispers into my ear. I nearly choke on my beer.

"What?" I turn to look at her.

"You heard. I want you to be my first. And I want you tonight." She leans forward and kisses me on the cheek. She then places her finger on my cheek and turns my face to hers. Leaning forward, she whispers, "You game?"

She kisses me on the lips, and before long, I'm under her spell again. I don't know what it is about her kisses, but she's addictive. She climbs up so that she's straddling me with her legs wrapped around my waist. "I want you so bad," she says as she kisses me again.

"We need to get out of here fast." I growl. I lift her off my lap, grab her hand, and almost run out of The Underground.

We jump in a taxi that's waiting outside and go to her place. She doesn't live too far from me, but I don't tell her that. When we get inside, as soon as she closes the door, I'm on her. I push her against the wall and devour her. My hands are touching her all over. I'm like a man starved of a woman.

She pulls back. "Let's go somewhere more comfortable," she says, taking my hand this time and leading me further into her apartment and into her bedroom.

It's only when I look at her now that I can see she's nervous. "Princess, we don't have to do this. We can just do other stuff. I don't want you to give me the best gift ever if it's not really something you want to do yet." I kiss her and the emotions flowing through my body send me in a tailspin. I need her so badly, but I need to let her guide me.

"Zac, I want you. I want you tonight."

I smile at her and then I approach her and pull her in tight for a hug. "I don't know what you do to me, Issy, but I need you so much." After running my hands all over her, I start to take her dress off. When it goes over her head, I stand back and look at her. She really is perfect. "You're gorgeous. What do you want with me? I'm a broken, damaged, and angry man, Issy. Why do you want me?"

She moves closer to me and starts to undo my shirt. "I want you because of those things. I know you're damaged and I want to fix you. I want to fill the void that you have. I want to be your best friend, your lover, your true love."

My shirt is on the floor with her dress and she reaches behind her back and undoes her bra, letting that slip to the floor too. I gasp; her tits look gorgeous. I lean forward and touch them and she throws her head back. I take one of them into my mouth and she runs her hands through my hair. "God, Zac, bite them."

I do and she squeals out loud. I love all the little reactions she's giving me, egging me on further.

Reaching back, I undo my trousers and leave them on the floor with the rest of our clothes. Now we're both standing in just our underwear. I get down on my knees and pull her towards me. She is tiny, so petite. I know I have to be gentle with her. I put both my hands on her panties and pull them down slowly. Then I reach in and cup between her legs. "God, Issy, you're wet for me."

"Of course I am. I want you." She watches me.

I lean against the bed and pull her so that she's bent over my head and then I open up her lips and lick her gently at first, but once I get a taste of her sweet honey, I start to speed up and lick her hard. I put one finger inside her. She cries out. Fuck, she's tight. I force another finger inside her; she feels so good.

My tongue is flicking her clit and I love the noises she's making. I'm controlling them and her. When she starts panting and I feel her body tense up, I slow down. I don't want her to have an orgasm yet. I want to see her face when she has her first one for me.

"Princess, I'm going to turn you over now and I'm going to finish you off properly. I want to watch your face when you come all over my tongue and fingers."

"Oh my God, Zac. Keep talking like that. I love it."

I chuckle and I know the vibration flows right through her body.

I move away from the bed and pick her up, kiss her, and then place her back down on the bed. "Lean up on your elbows so you can watch me," I command. She does everything I say.

Kneeling down again in front of her, I open her legs. She watches me plunge two fingers inside her. She watches me lick her pussy and her clit. I watch her body start to shudder.

"Fuck, Zac, I need to come," she says as she closes her eyes and throws her head back.

"Issy, look at me when you come, please. I need to see the emotions in your eyes."

She looks at me, and as I lick her pussy and plunge my fingers in and out, I look at her. We're staring into each other's eyes as she tenses for the last time and then she screams out loud. "Fuuuuuuck!"

I chuckle which sends her over the top completely. Watching her come apart was the most beautiful thing I've ever experienced.

I give her a few minutes to get her breath back and then I climb on the bed next to her and hold her tight. "That was amazing," I say to her. "You felt perfect around my fingers."

"Fuck, Zac. I've never had an orgasm like that."

"Then you've never met the right guy." I kiss her and I feel really emotional. I can feel myself falling for her; I can't help myself.

"I have now." She kisses me back.

After a while, she gets up and brings me a drink. We climb into her bed and she leans against me as we talk and drink. "Do you remember me?" she asks.

"I'll be honest. No, I don't. I don't remember much about those days. I was on a path of self-destruction and I didn't care who got in my way."

"I remember you."

"Really?"

"Yeah. I fancied you the first time I saw you. I was at The Underground with Damien and you were being loud and boisterous."

"Nothing new there then." I laugh.

"So true. You wanted to fight anyone and everyone,

and when you jumped in the ring you were like a true gladiator. I think I fell for your fighting first. Then you were taking home different girls every night, sometimes more than one."

"Yeah. As I said, they weren't the best days of my life."

"I tried to talk to you, but you didn't even see me. It's like you didn't like me enough to acknowledge me."

"I'm sorry, princess. It's probably good we didn't get together then. Nothing would have come of it."

"You think it will this time?" she says quietly. For all her bravado, she's really a scared girl.

"Who knows? But I know I want to try if you do. We have some sort of a connection that drives me insane and I'd love to pursue it."

She goes quiet for a while then puts both our drinks down and turns to me, straddles my lap, and says, "Fuck me, Zac. Please?"

How did I end up with this gorgeous girl asking me to do that? Did I die and go to heaven?

"Are you sure? Maybe it should be a bit more romantic, not when we've been drinking all day and night."

"Are you saying you can't perform, pretty boy?" She smiles as she jiggles up and down over the top of my hard cock.

"I'm going to ask you one more time. Do you really want to do this? Now is the time to back out. I know that once I'm inside you, I'll keep going until I've fucked you senseless."

She looks at me, smiles, and says, "I want that and then I want to do it all over again."

I don't wait for her to change her mind. I roll her off me and go to my jeans, take a condom out of my pocket and then drop my boxers. I hear her gasp. I'm not small and she's tiny so I can see her doing the maths. It's going to be tight.

I crawl over her body and spread her legs open. I sit back and put the condom over my cock and roll it down. She watches me eagerly. Then I kiss her. Our tongues are fighting for space and I run one of my hands down to knead her tit. She starts moaning and wriggling under me. Then I move down and kiss her tit and knead the other one. She is wriggling and moaning. I grab my cock and line it up. I know I need to go slow, and by God, I try to.

I inch my way in. She tenses up and her eyes go wide. "Oh my God," she says.

I inch in again. "You okay?"

"Uh huh." Her eyes are wide open.

"I'm not even half way in yet, princess," I say and smile as I push another inch in.

Her eyes widen. "You mean there's more?"

I look down and laugh. "Hell yeah there is." She looks down and sees my cock in her pussy and between us.

She gulps. "I don't think it will fit."

"Of course it will. I just need to go slow." I lean down and kiss her, and when I feel her relax, I push another inch in. She hasn't even noticed and I reach out and touch her tits. Then I lean down and take one of them into my mouth and when I bite down on her nipple I push another inch in.

"Oh my God. I feel full up."

I push past her barrier and all the way in. It's the only way. Go fast and the pain will disappear.

"Fuck, Zac. Stop!" she shouts. I relax inside her tight pussy. It's so tight I might lose feeling in my cock.

"Are you okay, princess? Do you want me to pull out?" I ask, crossing my fingers in case she says yes.

"No, just stop for a minute." She reaches up and grabs

my neck and brings my face down to hers. "Kiss me, make me forget the pain." We kiss for what seems like hours, but my cock is still inside her and I slowly move it out. She doesn't even notice. I push it back in.

Then when I try to take it out this time her hands reach down and grasp my arse. "Don't you dare take it out. Fuck me. I'm ready."

"Are you sure? I won't go hard tonight. But next time you are going to be fucked so hard you won't be able to get out of this bed."

"Do it!"

She doesn't need to ask me again. I pull all the way out of her and slam back in. She screams and scratches my back. That sends me insane. I lift her hips up so that I can go deeper and then I fuck her shamelessly.

She is screaming, scratching, and grabbing my arse. She starts to tighten under me and I can feel that she's close. Good, because so am I.

"Princess, let yourself go," I say as I pummel in and out of her. I reach down and use my thumb on her clit and it sends her over the edge. She starts bucking and screaming, "Fuuuuuck, Zac!" It sends me in a tailspin after her.

"Issy, fuck!"

It takes a while for my cock to stop pulsing and then I pull out slowly. She is laid out on the bed and she looks so beautiful. I climb out of the bed.

"Where the fuck are you going?" she says. "Do you really think you can fuck and run? I gave you my most precious possession, you can't leave me." She starts to cry.

"Chill, princess. I'm not leaving you." I lean over and kiss her. "I'm just going to get rid of the condom so I can climb in behind you and hold you tight. There's nothing like a post sex cuddle."

She nods and dries her eyes. "Sorry. I've always had

this fear that when I gave away my virginity, someone would take it and run."

I go into the bathroom and then come back out and climb into the bed next to her. "Not me, princess. I'm here and I'm not going anywhere. I want this to work as much as you do."

SEETHING JEALOUSY

*1 OZ SWEET VERMOUTH, ½ OZ WHISKEY, ½ OZ CHERRY
BRANDY, ½ OZ ORANGE JUICE*

Waking up the next morning, I wonder where I am. Then I feel a warm body lying in front of me and I remember Issy. She was amazing last night. I grab her and pull her close to me. "Morning, princess," I say, kissing her on the back of her neck.

"Mmm. Morning, pretty boy." She shuffles backwards until her arse touches my cock. "Ooh, hello. There's a broom in my bed." She laughs.

"How are you feeling? Are you sore?" I ask, running my hand down her stomach and between her legs.

"Mm, I don't know. Put a finger inside me and check."

I laugh. "Okay, princess." I run my finger between her lips and then thrust it inside her.

"Ow, yeah. That's sore," she says and I pull my finger out.

I roll her onto her back and I climb down her body and

kiss her between her lips with both her legs caressing my face.

Spreading her legs apart, I tongue between her lips and then I thrust my tongue inside. She doesn't moan like when my finger went inside, so that's good. I flick it back and forth and she starts bucking against my mouth. I use my nose to tickle her clit and I hold her lips open so that I get my tongue as deep as possible. I take my tongue out and then suck on her clit and she bucks hard against my face. "Zac, oh my God, I'm so close." I keep thrusting my tongue in and out and then sucking and flicking her clit.

She finally lets go and falls over the edge. I suck and suck on her clit and I can feel her twitching beneath me.

When she has calmed down, I climb up and kiss her. All of a sudden she pushes me over and straddles me.

"No, princess. You're too sore."

"Who says I want to fuck you?" She slides down my body, kissing my nipples and nipping at them and then kissing my abs until she gets to the 'V'. She follows the line until she's face to face with my cock. I hold my breath, hoping she's going to touch him or kiss him.

She takes hold of my cock and squeezes it. Then she sticks her tongue out and licks the pre-cum which has come out of the end while she was having her orgasm.

"Mmm, Zac, you taste good." She opens her mouth and takes me inside, inch after inch.

"Fuck, Issy. Keep doing that."

She giggles and the vibrations send me insane. She keeps taking more of my cock in her mouth until I feel myself hit the back of her throat. She's only small so her hand is still wrapped around the base of my cock and she moves it up and down while it's in her mouth.

She tries to open her throat and take me further, but I

hear her gag. I put my hand on her head gently and tell her, "You don't need to do that, princess. It's okay."

She pulls her mouth off. "I want to do that, but I think I need more practice." She smiles at me and tries again by taking all of my cock in her mouth.

She gags again and then she takes my cock out of her mouth and moves up a bit to take it between her tits and she starts wanking my cock with her tits. Wow, that feels amazing. Then she leans down and opens her mouth around the end of my cock and looks up at me.

Have you ever been between a woman's tits with her mouth around it? No? Well, let me tell you, you haven't lived. It feels amazing, but it looks even better.

"I can't hold on much longer, you sexy minx," I say, trying not to close my eyes. It's much better when I look.

"Come on, Zac. Give it to me. Get it in my mouth." She moves her mouth closer to the tip, lifting her eyes to look at me as she wanks my cock.

It doesn't take long before I'm shooting my load into her mouth, on her cheeks, her chin and of course her beautiful tits.

She looks so beautiful with my cum all over her. Wow, she has surprised me and exhausted me at the same time.

She licks me clean and then climbs up my body and collapses on top of me. "You'll wear me out," she says, kissing me.

We hold each other tight and fall asleep together.

A FEW HOURS LATER, we sit on the balcony, having breakfast and coffee, when she says, "So, what's your plans today?"

"I've got to go and face my family. I didn't turn up for

work last night and I got roasted at dinner for acting like a tit over you the other night."

"Did you really get into trouble? That's hilarious."

"No, it's not. I care what they think of me. So I need to go and smooth things over. I've been having a hard time recently and I've been taking it out on everyone else."

"Do you want to talk about it?" She takes a sip of her coffee.

"Not really. I'm not ready yet. Now, let's stop being morbid. What are your plans for the day?"

"Well, I was going to see if you wanted to spend the day with me, because I assume you're working tonight."

"Yeah, I am. I need to go to Mixology around five to help with an order so I'm free up to then if you want to do something."

Her eyes light up and she comes around to my side of the table and sits on my lap. She puts her arms around my neck and brings my head down so that we are eye to eye. "Is it mad that I want to spend every minute with you?"

I smile. "No. I feel the same." She leans forward and kisses me.

When we break apart, she leans her head against my chest while I drink my coffee. It feels so natural to have her hanging off me. When I was with Erika, we never did anything like that. We were both professionals and our relationship was passionate, but we didn't cuddle or just sit and look at each other. I want to touch Issy all the time; I never felt like that with Erika. It upsets me that I think about Erika in that way. She was my soulmate. She was my forever. Can a person have more than one soulmate in their life? Can this little, petite girl be my new soulmate? I don't know, but I am going to enjoy every minute until it's over. Because it will be over, one way or another.

"How do you fancy coming on the boat with me today?"

"You have a boat?'

"Yeah. Well, Damien has and I can use it whenever I want. Let's pack up some food and sail over to Dartmouth or something." I can see the excitement in her eyes.

"That sounds like a great idea. I need to ring Mum and smooth things over and then we can head out. I need to go home and change. Do you want to come with me?" I say, without even thinking.

"I'd love to." She leans up and kisses me before climbing off my lap and taking the dishes into the kitchen.

The first thing I do is ring Mum. She answers after three rings.

"Morning, Zac." She sounds pissed off.

"Morning, Mum. Sorry about yesterday. I don't know what's got into me. It's always hard at this time of year, you know."

"I know that, that's why I asked how you were doing. You know Sunday dinner is sacred in my house. All our fights are left at the door."

"I know and I'm sorry."

"I heard you didn't turn up for work last night. Are you sure everything is okay?"

I feel uncomfortable and feel about ten years old. "I went on a drinking binge."

I hear her gasp. "Zac, we are not going through that again, are we?"

"No, honest. I met up with Issy and we sorted things out." I smile.

"Okay. I'm a little bit dubious about this girl if she makes you have these feelings and makes you turn to drink already. It might be too explosive for me."

I walk outside. "It's not like that. I promise. She just

makes me feel again. Not only that, but she makes me feel alive."

"Well, then I will give her the benefit of the doubt, but I'm watching you both carefully."

"I know and, Mum, I'm sorry."

"I love you, Zac. Just take care of yourself."

"I will. I'm going to ring Hunter and go into work tonight."

"He might not be as easy as me to win round." She laughs.

"You mean you were easy?" I laugh. "God help me with Hunter then."

We hang up, and when Issy is ready, we jump into my car and drive to my house. I leave her to look around while I jump in the shower. Then, after getting dressed, I ring Hunter.

When he answers the phone I say, "Sorry. I've been struggling. You know I don't like to talk about things. I know I let you all down."

"Have you finished bullshitting me now?" Hunter says. "All I need to know is are you working tonight?"

Typical Hunter, never has much to say.

"Yeah. I'll be there at five to do the order."

"Great. See you then." He takes a breath. "Zac, you know I'm here if you need me." Then he hangs up before I get chance to say anything.

WE DIDN'T END up getting a picnic together. Instead, I took Issy to the floating restaurant in Dartmouth. I love it there; Mum and Dad used to take us there a lot when we were teenagers. It's so cool. You pull up at the side of the restaurant, dock your boat, and climb aboard. It feels so strange sitting and having dinner with a woman after all these years. Yet, at the same time, it feels normal.

"Your boat is gorgeous, Issy. How long has Damien had it?"

"He's had it about three years. He makes a lot of money from his fighting and decided he wanted something to show from it. He's been going to The Underground for about ten years. He progressed to some fights in London and that's where he made most of his money. Then he came back home and fights here. He still gets money because he's hard to beat but he doesn't really need to fight anymore. He does it to help Mum and Dad out."

"I remember fighting him a few years ago when I first moved back here. He really is a good fighter."

"Yeah, I saw you and Damien fighting. You managed to beat him down very quickly. No-one has ever done that again. He started making more money when you stopped fighting." She laughs. "That's why I was surprised to see you back. Your departure was abrupt and you weren't expected to be back. I heard you were there once a year, but it was never when I was there."

"Damien is a good guy and if he is doing it to help your parents, then that makes him even better, in my opinion. How will he react when he knows we're together?"

"Despite you beating him, he actually likes you and respects you. Are we together? Or did we just have sex?" She looks at me shyly.

"Well, that depends on what you want. I believe that because I was your first you'd want me to hang around. I want to be with you. I want to see where this goes." I reach across the table and take her hand. "What do you want, Issy?"

She visibly relaxes. "I want that too. I want to see where this goes." She leans over the table and kisses me.

"Time to pay and get on the boat." I growl and she laughs.

When we're sailing back to Torquay, I steer and she's standing beside me with my arm wrapped around her. Every now and again, I kiss her. We're comfortable with each other out here where no one can interrupt us.

"I'm working tonight. Are you coming down?"

"Are you going to let me in?" She smiles at me, looking all innocent.

"Of course I am. Just don't be dancing with any strange men."

She laughs. "Yeah. I'll be down around ten thirty. Damien has a fight first so I'll be there to support him then come down to see you." She kisses me and I slow the boat down. Once we've stopped, I move her to the back of the boat and sit down. She straddles my lap and kisses me. Her hands are in my hair and she is pulling it. She is a sex kitten.

"Zac, I want you inside me now," she says as she starts pulling my top off.

"You're sore," I say, helping her out of her bikini top.

"I don't care. Please. I want to feel you inside me."

We help each other out of our clothes, and after I've put a condom on, she straddles me again.

"You can control the depth and how fast or slow we go. You're in charge."

She nods and then slowly sinks down on my hard cock.

It feels like heaven. It's like coming home. She is so tight and she envelopes my cock with her velvet pussy.

"Oh my God. That is so much deeper than last night." She sits very still.

I tense my cock so that it moves inside her. She laughs. "What was that? Do it again."

I do and she laughs every time, then she starts tensing her muscles around my cock and my laughter stops.

"Are you just going to sit there or do I need to move you myself?" I growl.

She laughs. "I thought this was at my own pace."

"It is, but if you don't do anything in the next ten seconds, I am changing that rule."

She lifts herself up and then crashes back down. She screams, "Fuuuck," and then she starts wriggling her arse around and grinding against my cock.

I grab hold of her waist; I can't wait for her to keep teasing me and I start moving her up and down my cock. She has her fingers in my hair, tearing it from its roots. God, it feels so good when she does that. It makes me feel animalistic.

As she pulls my hair, she leans in and her tits are at the perfect height to go into my mouth. I take one of them and I suck on her nipple and hear her groan and throw her head back. She is really sensitive and I bite gently. She moans again. So I bite down hard and she screams, "Again. Oh my God, do that again."

I do and she loves it. Then I take the other tit and do the same; bite gently and then harder. I feel her squeezing my cock tight as she falls over the edge of her orgasm. I don't stop moving her up and down over my cock as she squeezes the life out of it. I slow down as she comes down from her high and then I thrust in another few times before I go overboard myself.

She sits on my lap and leans her forehead against mine. "Is this what it feels like all the time?"

"Not for me. This feels amazing. You're one in a million, Issy."

After sitting just staring into each other's eyes for a few

minutes, she climbs off and we get dressed. Then we sail back into the harbour and I drive her home.

"See you later, yeah?" I ask.

She kisses me. "Of course, pretty boy. Look forward to it."

IT'S eleven o'clock and we are really busy, but I notice Issy isn't here yet. "Are you sure she hasn't gone in yet?" I ask Ainsley.

"Yes. Don't you think she would have stopped and given you a kiss." She raises her eyebrows as if I'm stupid to think I had missed her going into the bar.

I text her:

Zac: Where are u? Are u coming down?

I stand watching the queue outside get longer. I poke my head out the door to see if she being stupid and standing in the queue. Nope, she's not there.

I start to panic. Where the fuck is she? I text her again.

Zac: Where are u? What are u doing? Who are u doing?

I need to know where she is and that she's okay. All my insecurities and worries about Erika start to run through me. I feel cold and shiver.

I get a text about half an hour later.

Issy: What the fuck does that mean?

Zac: Where the hell are u Issy? I'm worried.

Issy: Really? I'm not even an hour late and u already think that I'm with someone else. Wtf?

Zac: When I make plans, I keep them.

She is really pissing me off. I put my phone in my pocket and concentrate on the queue of people coming into the bar.

Next thing, I hear is, "Zac we need you at the bar."

I rush into the bar and up to Keaton to see what's going on. There is a guy who is clearly off his face drunk, trying to get another drink, but failing.

"We won't serve him another drink. He's had too many already," Keaton says.

"Right, come on. It's time to leave. You've had enough tonight. Go home and sleep it off." I grab him by the arm and try to pull him away from the bar.

"Get lost!"

That is like hanging a red rag in front of me, especially with the mood I'm in.

"Come on. I think you need to go before we have to carry you out," I say, dragging him behind me.

He stands still and won't budge. I go up behind him and grab his elbow and pull him with me through the bar. He starts shouting at me. To be honest, I don't understand a lot of what he says as he's slurring so much.

When I get him outside, I pull him close to me and say, "Go home and sleep it off. But don't think you can come back in this state again." I push him gently in the direction of the taxis.

"Wanker!" he says as he wanders down the road, swaying from side to side.

When I get back inside, I check my phone to see if Issy has replied. Oh, yeah. She has definitely replied.

Issy: Really? U think because I'm late I don't want to see u. Well right now you're right. Fuck u Zac.

About five minutes later there's another text.

Issy: Ignoring me now are u? Well that's really mature.

Then a few minutes later.

Issy: I'm not coming down to see you tonight. I've had a better offer. See you around prick!

What the fuck? Now she has really pissed me off. A better offer? What does she mean by that? Now that's she's not a virgin she thinks she can give her pussy to anyone. She used me to lose her virginity and now she wants to spread it around. Well, that's fucking great, isn't it?

I man the door while Ainsley has her break and I'm stewing on Issy's words. All I can see is red and I turn away so many people because they look like they will piss me off.

"Well, look at the fucking face on you," Ainsley says. "No wonder there's no punters coming in. You look like you lost a tenner and found a penny."

"Leave it."

She laughs. "Trouble in paradise already?"

"Yeah. She got a better offer."

"Oh dear."

I can't wait for tonight to be over. I feel like I want to go to The Underground and fight someone, but I know that isn't the answer to everything. And, she might be there anyway.

When we have got rid of the last customer and tidied up, I leave. "See you all tomorrow," I say, walking to my car.

"Don't dwell on it, Zac. I'm sure she's fine," Ainsley says. "She'll come round tomorrow. I know she likes you a lot."

"Why the hell would you say that? She was late to meet me and then told me she had a better offer."

"I'm sure you gave her good reason to say that to you. You weren't in the best of moods tonight."

I drive my car hard, breaking lots of speed limits as I go. I'm so angry at Issy for telling me she had a better offer. But I'm mad at myself for chasing her. She doesn't know what happened to Erika. It's not her fault it's left me emotionally scarred and worried if someone is late. I even have a fit if someone in my family is late.

Climbing out of the car, I see Issy sitting on my doorstep.

"What the fuck are you doing out here at this time of night?" I ask, walking up to her.

When she looks up at me, I can see she's been crying. I lean down, pick her up, and cradle her in my arms. "What happened? Are you hurt?" I ask, kissing her on the head.

"No. You're a prick." She sobs, but she doesn't fight me holding her. I somehow manage to open the front door and bring her inside. When we get into the lounge, I put her down on the couch and kneel down beside her.

I take her head in my hands and kiss her on the lips. "Has someone hurt you, Issy?"

"Only you." She sobs. That's when my heart breaks in two. How could I do that to her? Why did I say those things to her?

"I'm sorry. I'm really sorry. I have my own issues and I find it hard to deal with someone being late."

"You didn't have to say those horrible things to me though. You could have rung me and spoken to me."

"I was working. It was busy. I was expecting to see you. I was looking forward to seeing you. I want to be with you all the time and it freaks me out when you're away from me."

"That's being a bit obsessive Zac. I am my own woman and I like time to myself as well. Don't smother me or we won't make it."

"I want to make it. I want to make this work," I say, holding her chin up. When she lifts her eyes to look into mine, I can see how much I hurt her. It kills me. "Princess, forgive me. I shouldn't have acted the way I did."

"Neither should I." She giggles.

"What are we going to do, Issy?" I kiss her on the lips and devour her. She puts her hands around my neck and pulls me closer, tugging at my hair.

When she pulls away, she yawns.

"Do you want me to take you home, or do you want to stay with me tonight?"

"Can I stay with you? I want to be close to you tonight. I want to know that you want me."

"I'll always want you, princess. Come on. Let me take you to bed."

Picking her up, I carry her to the bedroom where I undress both of us and then we climb into bed. I'm not going to fuck her tonight. I'm not going to fuck her tonight. I have to keep telling myself that so that I don't fuck her. I want to prove to her that I want her, not just for sex.

She starts to fall asleep and I pull her in as close as she will go. "Night, princess. Sorry."

"Night, pretty boy. Sorry."

I smile and we both fall asleep.

BEGINNING OF THE END

1 ½ oz Cahaca, ¼ oz Amaretto, ¾ oz Lime Juice, ½ oz Simple Syrup, ½ Egg White

I'VE BEEN SEEING Issy for a few weeks now and I'm really happy. She has crept under my skin and set up home there. We're together every single night, either at her place or mine. We've been to The Underground, but I'm not fighting and I've met her brother again. He's a decent guy and he told me that he only started making real money once I left.

Issy comes down to Mixology when I'm working and she gets on really well with the girls. Ainsley is a bit suspicious of her, because she sees how I am when she's late or we have an argument, which we do quite a lot. Scarlett and Dakota find her really funny and they have had some nights out together.

We argue a lot. It makes our relationship passionate and we love make up sex. Issy was always adventurous and she has been especially adventurous in the bedroom, bathroom, balcony or wherever we have sex. I feel differently for her than I did with Erika. I always thought Erika was my other half, my ying to her yang, and our relationship was always special. But my feelings for Issy are off the charts. The only downside is that I need to know where she is at all times. I haven't explained my reasons and sometimes she says I'm worse than Christian Grey. If she goes anywhere, I need her to text me when she leaves, when she gets there, and periodically through the evening. This is what causes most of our arguments, and the fact that I am insanely jealous of her talking to other guys.

Tonight is no exception, but this time I take it too far. As usual.

I'm working tonight and there is a big group of stag parties coming in. Issy is with me, talking, when they come in.

Ainsley lets them in, and before they go into the bar, I say, "Now, lads, we don't want any trouble. At the first sign of any one of you causing any trouble, you will all be asked to leave."

"Yeah, no problem. Understood," the best man says and they make their way into the bar. They are laughing and having a joke, and now and again, I can hear them.

"Hey, pretty boy, I'm going to get a drink," Issy says. She still calls me pretty boy. It always makes me laugh.

"Great. Would you get me and Ainsley a coffee while you're at it? Pretty please?" I wiggle my eyebrows.

She laughs. "You know I can't resist you when you do that." She leans up and kisses me. Her kisses are still addictive.

I slap her on the arse when she walks past me into the bar.

"She's lovely," Ainsley says. "She's very funny." She smiles at me.

"Yeah, I know. That's one of the things I love about her."

"You love her?"

"I didn't mean it like that," I say, backtracking slightly. I think about it. Do I love her? I think I do. I want to be with her all the time. She makes me smile when I'm with her. I can't imagine my life without her. Yeah, I think I do love her.

We have a really busy spell at the front door and it's about forty minutes later when we can breathe again that I realise Issy hasn't been back out with our coffees.

"Hey, Ains. I'm going to see where Issy is with our coffees. I won't be long."

"No problem. I could do with that coffee right now. My hands are freezing."

"See you in a bit." I open the door into the bar. As soon as I open the door, the music hits me. Skylar is doing a great job tonight; the dancefloor is full. I look to see if Issy is dancing. She loves dancing and sometimes gets carried away with herself and dances in a corner on her own. No, she's not there.

As I make my way from the dancefloor to the bar to see if she is talking to Dakota or Keaton, I hear her laughing. Turning, I see her leaning her back against a wall with one leg kicked up behind her and some guy is leaning towards her with one hand on the wall behind her.

I don't even stop to ask questions. I waltz right over there and pull him away from her.

"Zac, what the fuck are you doing?" she shouts.

"Yeah, man. What are you doing? I wasn't causing any trouble." I see it's the best man from earlier.

"That's my girlfriend you're hitting on," I spit at him as I try to pull him out of the bar.

"I wasn't hitting on her. We were talking about the wedding in a couple of weeks. I'm married. I'm not interested in your girlfriend." He holds his hands up in the air.

"Get the fuck out of my bar!"

He lunges at me and tries to hit me. I laugh at him because he's small in comparison to me.

I take his hand, wrap it around his back, and march him out of the bar. When I get him outside, his mates have followed and I shout to him, "Stay the fuck away from the bar and my girlfriend."

"I don't know what she's doing with you anyway. You're a fucking fruit loop. You shouldn't be working in a bar when all you want to do is cause trouble." The best man squares up to me.

He really picked the wrong person to square up to tonight. I'm ready for a fight. I punch him in the face and he goes down. What I'm not ready for is his mates all coming at me at the same time.

Everything happens at once. Issy comes out screaming at me. The ten guys from the stag party all start hitting me. One of them has a knife and I don't even see it coming. He jabs me in the stomach and I can feel the blood slowly trickling out over my t-shirt.

When I fall to the floor, they all start kicking me. I hear screaming. I'm not sure if it's Issy, Ainsley, or both. Then I hear Hunter and Keaton coming out and trying to get the stag party to stay. I hear someone say there is an ambulance on the way and then I hear shouting at the stag party, so I can only assume they have run off.

A FEW HOURS LATER, I wake up and I'm in a hospital

bed. There's a lot of beeping of machines and it hurts when I move. Mum is sitting next to the bed, and when I move slightly, she wakes up. I can see she's been crying and she leans over me and hugs me gently. "Zac, you're going to be okay." She kisses me. "You were lucky."

I'm groggy. I don't feel lucky.

"What happened?" I manage to ask.

"You were knifed and it went straight through your spleen. You had to have an operation. You could have bled out. Luckily, the ambulance was close by and got you here quickly." She takes my hand.

All that goes through my mind is that I wonder if Erika suffered. Did she feel the blood trickling out of her body? She didn't die instantly. Was she in pain? I start to cry.

"Zac, what's wrong? You're going to be okay." She presses a button on the side of my bed and then she stands over me and rubs her hand down my face.

"Erika."

"What about her?" she asks, confused.

"I wonder if she was scared. Was she in a lot of pain? Did she think of me? How did she feel as she was dying?"

"Zac, stop!" Mum says harshly. "Don't torture yourself about that night. You have got to stop this. You've been dealing with the guilt for five years and you are taking your anxieties out on Issy. You have her driven demented. She doesn't understand."

"I know. I feel so guilty though, Mum. I killed her."

"NO! You didn't. The driver did."

I sob. "But... I was talking to her and complaining that she was late as usual. She was listening to me and not looking where she was going. It's my fault." I break down sobbing. I've never told anyone before that I blame myself for her death.

Just then the nurse comes in. "Ah, you're awake, Mr

James. You've been through a traumatic experience and we will be keeping you in for a few days. You gave everyone a scare, you know? You've had a lot of people pacing up and down the corridors all night." I look at Mum and she gives me a little wry smile.

"I don't want to see anyone, Mum. Please?"

"I think you should see Issy. She is so worried about you." She touches my hand.

"I can't see her. Especially not her." I cry again and shake my head.

The nurse looks at Mum. "Is he okay?"

"Not really. He has never come to terms with the death of his girlfriend five years ago and this incident has brought it all to the surface. Can he have something to make him sleep so he doesn't think about it?"

She nods. "I'll go and check with the doctor and then I'll be right back."

Before she goes, she places her hand on my arm. "I can get someone to talk to you about grief counselling. It will make you feel better." She leaves the room and I look at Mum. She's smiling at me.

"It will make you feel better if you talk about it with someone. You should tell Issy. She might understand you a bit better. Your relationship is very volatile and destructive and I fear that if you don't tell her how you feel then something terrible is going to happen. If you love her, you need to talk to her about it."

"I know, but I don't know how I feel about it all. Maybe I should just leave her. I don't deserve to be happy after what I did to Erika. Is the same thing going to happen to Issy? Maybe she'd be better off without me."

"Zac! Stop that right now. No one is going to be better off without you," Mum shouts before she starts sobbing.

The door opens and Hunter comes barging in. "What

the fuck is going on? Mum, are you okay?" He takes her into a hug.

She nods. "Yeah. But he's not." She points at me. "Hunter, he needs help. He's self-destructive."

He hugs her for a few minutes and then says, "Mum can you leave us for a couple of minutes?"

She nods and goes to leave the room. "The nurse is coming back with some tablets to help him sleep."

"No problem. I won't be long."

When Mum leaves, she closes the door, giving us some privacy.

"Zac, I know you went through the fucking mill five years ago. We went through it with you. We went through it again for three years until you sorted yourself out. Your relationship with Issy seems to be the catalyst in your recent behaviour. You need to sort yourself out or you need to get rid of her."

"It's not her fault I'm like this. It's me, Hunter. I don't deserve to be happy. I killed Erika. I don't have the right to be happy again. I panic when I don't know where Issy is. When she's late, it drives me insane with worry. I try not to show it, but inside it's killing me and all I can think about is that I'm going to get a call to say she was in an accident." I start sobbing again. I can't help myself and I don't care what my brother thinks.

"Have you been keeping these feelings to yourself all this time?"

I nod.

"We are a family and a fucking strong one at that. Why haven't you let us help you?"

"I needed to admit it to myself first."

He leans down and hugs me as the nurse comes back in.

"I have your tablets here. There's a young lady outside

who is causing quite a scene because she wants to come and see you." She smiles.

"I don't want her to come in and see me. Hunter, don't let her in." I shake my head vigorously.

He reaches out and takes my hand. "No one is going to make you do anything you don't want to do. I promise. But you will need to see her at some stage."

"I know. I'm just not up to it right now."

"I know."

The nurse gives me the tablets, and after about twenty minutes of sitting silently with Hunter, I feel my eyes start to close.

As Hunter leaves the room, I hear Issy asking to see me. I don't hear his reply as he closes the door and I fall asleep.

I'M GOING HOME TODAY. I've been in the hospital for a week, recuperating from my operation. During that time, I've had extensive grief counselling. I didn't think it would help, but it has tremendously. I've told the doctor that I think it's my fault and they've made me see that, actually, it isn't my fault. The driver who killed her was drunk and she was in the wrong place at the wrong time. Yes, she might have been on the phone to me, but it's not my fault.

They've put me on anti-depressants and have told me that they will take about two weeks to kick in and then I will start to feel better. I didn't want to take them. I feel like a failure for having to take them. But if they make me feel better in the long run, then I'm game.

Issy has been here every day to come and see me. I haven't let her in. I've told the nurses and the doctors that I don't want her to come in and speak to me. I'm not ready to face her and tell her what I did. I know now it's not my fault, but I'm scared of how she will feel about me.

I'm not going to be able to keep avoiding her when I leave the hospital though. I'm moving in with Mum and Dad for a week and then I'm going home.

I hope she waits for me to feel better, but I understand if I've pushed her too far away.

KISS ON THE LIPS

1 ½ OZ WHITE RUM, 1 OZ TRIPLE SEC, 4 ½ OZ RASPBERRY JUICE, ½ TBSP. GRENADINE, ICE

IT'S time for me to go back to my own house. Mum and Dad have been amazing, as I knew they would be. I don't wake up at night screaming as I remember what happened to Erika. I had nightmares when it first happened, but they went away. They've come back with a vengeance since my incident. Thankfully, they've finally stopped and I feel like I'm getting back to normal. I'm still sore from the operation and know that I can't go to the gym yet, or fight.

My family have all been very supportive and they didn't understand everything I was going through. They've all said that I should have talked to them. Maybe I should, but I didn't and I can't change that now. What I can do is talk to them now if I feel that way inclined. I'm still seeing the grief counsellor and it's helping me so much.

I'm ready to see Issy now. If she still wants to see me.

She hasn't been around the last couple of days. I might have pushed her too far away.

Dad drives me back to my house and helps me in with my bags. "Are you sure you're going to be okay, son? You can stay as long as you like with us, you know?"

"I know. Thanks, Dad, but I've got to get on with my life. I'm not going back to work for a while, so I'm just going to relax and enjoy life for a few weeks."

He smiles and then hugs me. "I'll see you for Sunday dinner this week."

"You sure will. I can't wait."

"Ainsley brought some food over for you. It's in the fridge."

"Thanks for everything, Dad."

He hugs me and then leaves.

It's so quiet in my house. Before all of this happened, the only thing I could hear in here was Issy's voice. Now, it's so bloody quiet.

I watch TV for a while and then sleep on the couch. It's nice to just exist without having the guilt eating me up.

My phone beeps with a text. I check it. It's Issy. She has sent me messages all day every day, but not for the last few days. So, I'm a little surprised to see one now.

Issy: Welcome home Zac. Hope u are feeling better. Miss you xx

Those last two words and kisses bring tears to my eyes. I don't know what will become of the two of us, but I owe it to her to see her to explain myself.

I text her back. This is the first time I have replied to any of her text messages since that night.

Zac: Thank u. Miss you too xx

Issy: Are u okay? Xx

Zac: Better than I was. I owe u an explanation, if u want one.

She doesn't reply straight away. I can feel my anxiety levels rise, but then I take a few deep breaths and I feel calmer. Just because she isn't replying straight away, it doesn't mean anything has happened to her. I just need to remember that.

About twenty minutes later, someone knocks on my front door. I make my way to the door and, when I open it, Issy is standing on the other side. God, she's beautiful. How have I managed to push her away for so long? As soon as I see her, I know I'm deeply and madly in love with her. I step to one side to let her in.

"Hi," I say.

"Hi."

We walk into the lounge and sit on the couch.

"Do you want a drink?" I ask.

She shakes her head and I can see she's been crying. The thought that I've made her cry hurts more than I thought it would.

We're both quiet and then she speaks very softly. "You said you owe me an explanation. I've been waiting for two weeks for one, so please talk to me."

I take a deep breath and then I tell her my story. "Five years ago, my life changed drastically. My girlfriend, Erika, was a designer and she was always running late. This particular night was our anniversary and we were supposed to have dinner in a beautiful restaurant. I was going to ask her to marry me. But she was running late, as usual. She wasn't answering her text messages or picking up her phone. Eventually, when I rang her, she answered and she was just locking up her studio. I was telling her off for being late and saidit was important she hurried up." I can see she's upset that I was going to ask Erika to marry me. She nods for me to continue.

"She was telling me she was running to get a taxi and

then, all of a sudden, she wasn't answering me. I was shouting and I heard a lot of screaming and eventually someone spoke to me." I take a deep breath and nearly jump out of my skin when she places her hand on my knee.

"Go on, if you can. You don't have to tell me. You don't owe me anything."

"I want to tell you. I need to tell you so that we can move on from this. Even if we don't do it together." I look in her face when I say that just to gauge her reaction, but I don't see anything there.

"A guy came on the phone and told me there had been an accident and I needed to get to the hospital. He asked me her name and any information I could give him. When I got to the hospital she was in a really bad way. They had told me to prepare for the worst. But who can do that? You've always got to have hope, right?" She nods her head. Tears flowdown her face. She knows what's coming next.

"They eventually let me in to see her and I was nearly sick. There were tubes everywhere. There was blood everywhere. They took her to the operating theatre and she died." Issy sobs. "She died on the table. She had too much internal bleeding and they couldn't control it. She died." I take a deep breath. "I blamed myself for her death for five years, Issy. I killed her. It's my fault she's dead."

"No, it's not, Zac. It's not your fault at all."

"Yes, it was. She was talking to me and I was rushing her. I didn't see a grief counsellor when it happened. I drank myself into oblivion and started fighting in London. Then, one day, my brothers came to London and dragged my sorry arse home. That's when I started going to The Underground and fighting and drinking all the time. Once again, my brothers intervened and made me see what I was doing to myself. Every year on her anniversary, I go to

The Underground, fight and drink and then don't go back."

"I see. I wondered why you only came once a year."

"I know now that it wasn't my fault she died. I see that. Being with you has made all my old feelings come to the surface. When I didn't hear from you or you were late, I would automatically assume you were dead."

"What?"

"Yeah. In my head, if you didn't answer your text right away, then you were dead. I couldn't handle anything happening to you. So instead of loving you and hugging you when I got to see you, I would lose the plot and start calling you names and whatever else just to get those feelings out of me. I'm sorry that I took it out on you. I hope one day you forgive me." I take her hand and bring it to my mouth and kiss it. I close my eyes and breathe her in.

She's sobbing.

"I'm madly in love with you, Issy, and when I saw that guy talking to you, I was so worried I was going to lose you and I couldn't handle that. I shouldn't have jumped to conclusions and I'm very sorry for the things I said and did that night. But I truly believe those things saved my life. I was on a path of self-destruction and I was bringing you with me. That was selfish and I see that now. I know you wouldn't have gone off with that guy, and if I had had time to think about it, I would have known you wouldn't, but those fears kept rising in me."

I look at her. She doesn't say anything, but tears are flowing down her face. I wipe them up with my thumb and then I put my thumb in my mouth to suck her tears away.

"I hope you understand what was going through my mind and know why I reacted the way I did. I hope you forgive me for trying to take you with me."

"Of course I forgive you, pretty boy," she says, sobbing.

"Thank you. You're an amazing woman and I know you'll be happy. I'm just sorry for hurting you."

Neither of us says anything for about ten minutes. We're both looking at the floor. "So, what happens now?" she asks meekly.

"That's up to you, Issy. I totally understand if you don't want to see me again and you can walk right out of here now. I'm just glad of the opportunity to tell you my side of the story and it might help you to understand me better."

"What if I don't want to walk out of here right now? What happens then?"

I look up quickly. Is she saying she wants to try to make it work? No way, she can't be.

"What? What... What do you want to do then?" I ask.

"I don't want to walk out of here. What kind of woman leaves her man when he needs her the most? I understand what you went through and it fucking sucks balls. I understand how that has shaped the last five years of your life. But you have me now and we can get through anything. You and me can deal with anything life throws at us. But the only way that is going to work is if we work as a team." She moves in front of me and climbs on my lap. I hold my breath; I don't want to read too much into it.

"I'm madly in love with you too, Zac. Even with your flaws and strange ways. I understand them now. It all makes sense. But the one thing I know is that the last two weeks have been absolute hell without you. I've tried every trick in the book to see you in the hospital and then your parents must have been fed up with getting rid of me from their door. I just hope they still like me."

"Of course they do. Who wouldn't?"

"I want you, warts and all. We're in this together, Zac. If we're going to make a go of this, then we have to do this together. It's the only way it's going to work. So, no going caveman on me. We talk about everything and we work it out. Together. Do you hear me?"

I nod. "Yes. I hear you, princess."

She smiles. "I thought I'd never hear you call me that again." She leans forward and places a very gentle kiss on my lips. I wrap my arms around her and hold her close to me.

We both cry for a while and when we finish, she kisses me again. This time I can't stop myself, I kiss her back. It feels amazing to have her in my arms again and I never want to let her go. I know that I have to and I have to let her do her own thing without me breathing down her neck all the time. Finally, I think I'm capable of doing that. I really do.

We go to bed and hold each other tight all night. I wake up a few times and whisper in her ear, "I love you so much, Issy."

I'm sure I hear her wake and say, "Right back at ya, Zac."

EPILOGUE

ISABELLA

So much has happened in the last few months that I feel utterly drained. Zac coming into my life, being such a big part of it, then the thought that I had lost him forever nearly killed me. Everything is good again now. When he moved home two weeks ago, I went round that first night and I've not been home since. Well, that's not true. Zac's house is my home and that's where I belong.

Zac has done so well. He's still seeing the grief counsellor once a week and that is going to be changing to once every two weeks and then once a month soon. It really helps him, but what helps him the most is talking to me about Erika and his life in the five years since she died. At first I found it hard to see him so upset about her, but then I realised that he loves me differently to the way he loved her. We are totally different people and our love has no boundaries.

We're going to his parents' for dinner. It's not the usual Sunday dinner, which I have to say is gorgeous, and I was made very welcome. Tonight is Keaton and Dakota's leaving dinner. They are off to Australia tomorrow for three months for the World Surfing Championships. They are amazing surfers and a wonderful couple. We're hoping to get out to see them while they're in Australia. It's one of those bucket list places, and while family is there, it's the perfect opportunity to go.

We get to their house and walk in. "Hi, we're here," Zac says.

"In here," their mum says.

Someone hands me a glass of prosecco as I walk into the lounge. I take it, but know I won't drink it. Zac is still on his anti-depressants and he can't drink alcohol, so I don't either. His mum hugs me and whispers in my ear, "It's only lemonade." She winks at me and gives Zac a hug. I smile. She has made me feel so welcome. I was worried that after the explosive start to our relationship, they wouldn't like me and they would hold me responsible for Zac's breakdown. But none of them have. They have all welcomed me with open arms and I truly feel a part of their family.

I've spent a good bit of time with Ainsley, Scarlett, and Dakota, and I know that we are all going to miss Dakota when she leaves.

"Hey, are you excited?" I ask when I walk over to the corner where the girls are all talking.

"Yeah, but I'm so nervous at the same time. I'm worried about Mum and leaving her on her own."

"I know, but you know Mum won't leave her on her own. She will be joining us for Sunday dinner at least once a month. And she will be going out to Australia with Mum and Dad," Ainsley says.

"I know, and that makes me feel so much better."

"So, Ainsley," Scarlett says, "it's your turn next."

"What do you mean? To go to Australia?"

Scarlett laughs. "No. To find a guy and settle down."

"Huh, that's not going to happen any time soon. Have you seen how over-protective my brothers are?" She laughs.

We all know what she's talking about. "Did you see what Hunter did when that guy was talking to me at the bar?"

"Yeah, he hovered by him and kept interrupting when he was talking," Scarlett says, laughing.

"Exactly my point. Zac keeps distracting anyone who talks to me at the front door too."

"They are a little bit protective over you," I say, smiling at her.

"A LITTLE BIT? It's got so bad, I've started to tell them I like girls, just so they will leave me alone."

"Oh my God, no way," I say, laughing.

Scarlett and Dakota start laughing too.

"No, seriously, girls, I have. They don't give me a minute's peace about the guys, so I thought if I told them I'm a lesbian, they'll back off."

"And are you?" Scarlett asks.

"No way. I like cock as much as you do," she says with a serious face.

It's too much for us to cope with and the four of us burst out laughing.

Zac comes over and puts his arm around my shoulders, pulls me into his body, and kisses me on the side of my head. "What's so funny, girls?"

That sends us into kinks of laughter and none of us can explain it to him. He stands there shaking his head, then says, "Okay then. I'll leave you girls to it." He walks away.

"Girls, I'm going to miss you so much. You're the sisters I never had," Dakota says with tears in her eyes.

"We're going to miss you too," Ainsley says. "Group hug."

The four of us hug each other and make promises to text and chat all the time while she's away.

After a couple of hours, I can see Zac is tired so I go over to him and wrap my arms around his waist and hug him tight. "Are you ready, pretty boy? I think it's time to go."

He smiles down at me and kisses me on the lips. "You're right, as usual."

He turns to Keaton and Dakota, giving them both hugs and says, "Good luck over there. Between the two of you, I know you'll bring some silverware home and wipe the floor with everyone else."

After saying goodbye to everyone, we leave and make our way home.

"I had a great time," I say to Zac when we're home and on the balcony. "I love your family."

"Our family, princess. My family is your family. You are one of us. One day you'll have the James' name too."

"I love you, Zac, do you know that? Sometimes I love you so much it physically hurts."

"I know how you feel. I'm sorry for everything I put you through." He looks so sad.

"We are so much stronger because of it," I say, hugging him.

"Yeah, we are. We're strong together."

We're silent for a while and then I climb on his lap and say, "Come on, pretty boy. Show me how much you love me."

And, of course, he does.

THE END

THANK you for reading ZAC as part of the Mixology Series. I really hope you enjoyed it and that you'll consider leaving a review on Amazon. It's a great way to help other readers discover new books.

Continue reading for a sneak peak of AINSLEY, the next book in the Mixology Series.

AINSLEY

Keaton and Dakota left this morning. I know we're going to see them soon, but it was really emotional saying goodbye. I love Dakota like a sister and Keaton is okay as a brother, I suppose. I'm hoping we can all go out and watch the World Championship, but I'm not sure we can organise something with Mixology. We'll have to wait and see. I'm sitting at the breakfast table looking out at the sea. I love the sea, it is so calming and it reminds me my childhood.

With my hands wrapped around my coffee I laugh as I remember telling the girls that I've told my brothers that I prefer girls. They have become so overprotective. They were always bad when we were growing up, but now it's out of hand. I can't have any dates because they find out about them. It's driving me insane. I've even gone so far as thinking of hiring a prostitute because I seriously need to get laid!

I can't dwell on it though as there is a lot of paperwork to do in Mixology. With Keaton leaving, the extra work needs to be spread out with Hunter taking on some extra jobs and Scarlett and I doing extra admin.

I love working with Scarlett, we always have so much fun and her relationship with Hunter is so good. They are well suited to each other. I'm happy they got together, even with what happened with Finn.

"Hey Scarlett," I say flinging my bag down on the desk. "What do we need to do today?"

"There's some bills that need paying and some orders that need placing. We've been really busy lately so we are going to have to chip in with bar work as well now that Dakota and Keaton have left us."

"Right let's write some lists and see how we get on with them." I love my lists. I write lists of lists that need to be written, if that makes sense.

When the delivery comes I rush outside because the driver is really nice.

"Hey Rod, how's things?" I say flirting with him. He's kind of sexy, in a dirty kind of way.

"Hey Ainsley. Looking better now I've seen you," he says picking up two of the barrels and carrying them on his shoulders so that I can see his muscles rippling.

Hunter comes out, "Ains, we'll organise the delivery, you can go back inside."

"No, it's fine, I just want to check some stuff with Rod. You can go back in, it's fine really." He is pissing me off now. I've been trying to talk to Rod for weeks now, but every time he's here one of my brothers comes out and takes over. It pisses me off.

"Ains," he says looking at me.

"Oh for god's sake!" I say storming off.

Scarlett starts laughing when I get into the office and slam the door. "I think you need to ramp up operation lesbian." She says.

"Who are you telling? I need sex Scarlett, like seriously

need it. I'm sick of using my vibrator all the time. Me and porn hub have a special relationship."

Scarlett is rolling around the place laughing, I think I even see tears in her eyes.

The door opens and Issy walks in. "What did I miss bitches?"

"Ainsley was just telling me that she needs sex and is fed up of using her vibrator!"

"Oh my god no way! Ainsley I can fix you up with someone if you want. I have some connections down The Underground!"

"Really that would be awesome." I say smiling at her. I'm not fussy at this stage.

Scarlett laughs, "Erm did you forget Zac goes down there. There is no chance he is going to let you hook up with anyone down there. No way in hell!"

"Fuck, I didn't think of that. Right I'm starting operation lesbian tonight. I've had enough. Then I'm going to find some guy who doesn't come here and doesn't know any of my brothers. Don't ask me how I'm going to do it, because I don't know myself. But I'm sure I can write a list for it."

The three of us break down laughing.

The boys come in. "What's going on here?" Zac asks.

"You don't want to know Pretty Boy!" Issy says.

I think it's hilarious that he lets her get away with calling him Pretty Boy. Keaton tried it one day and Zac tackled him to the floor. These guys are like five year olds. Seriously!

Zac picks Issy up and kisses her. He has no shame, he even touches her arse up in front of us. I want to be sick because, like, he's my brother, but damn it's hot.

Scarlett watches me and starts shaking her head and laughing.

"Fuck you all," I say and storm out of the office.

AINSLEY IS COMING on **Fall 2018**.

If you like ZAC and would like to read more, turn the page for a list of my other books. And if you don't want to miss any future releases, please join my Newsletter

Also by Krissy V

EROTIC ROMANCE

The Lust Train – Newsletter Exclusive Standalone

MIXOLOGY Series

Hunter

Keaton

Zac

DARK ROMANCE

My One Regret - Standalone

WHISKEY SOUR Series

Whiskey

Snow

TILL DEATH US DO PART Series

Till Death Us Do Part – Trilogy (For Better or For Worse, In Sickness and In Health, To Love and To Cherish)

To Have or To Hold – Standalone in Till Death Us Do Part Series

For Richer or For Poorer – Standalone in Till Death Us Do Part Series

CHOCOLATE BOX ROMANCE

Beauty Within

EFF THIS
DIET
someone give me fries

KRISSY V

Sneak Peek of Eff This Diet

D ear Readers

AS ALWAYS THIS IS HARD! I wrote this book originally for an anthology – Life After Losing.

I was listening to Mika's song, *You Are Beautiful*, and the subject of this book came into my mind. It is a very personal subject to me as I have struggled with my weight in the last five years.

I take medication which made me put on weight originally, now my eating habits aren't great and I still take the medication so it seems the chances of being a 'skinny minny' again are *slim!*

I shed many tears during the writing this book, not because it's sad – because it's not. But because I felt like I was in therapy and wanted to stand up and say, "My name is Krissy V and I am fat!"

So, I think firstly I need to thank myself for being so

honest and putting pen to paper to write about something that means a lot to me. I don't want anyone to think I am fat shaming – because I'm not.

I am Kayleigh in this story. She is me!

Most people can relate to Kayleigh and her weight struggles and I hope you understand her like I do!

Thank you all

Krissy V

Sneak Peek of Eff This Diet

"DARRAGH, I'm off to Fat Club. I'll see you later," I shout, as I head out the door. I don't hear his reply.

Darragh is one of my roommates. He's six foot two inches, gorgeous, and I love him. We're really close. Do I have feelings for him? Am I attracted to him? Hell yeah! I have a pulse, of course I'm attracted to him. I think even a nun would be attracted to him.

Do you know what makes him more attractive? He's a really nice guy. Like, seriously 'nice'. He would help anyone, he would do anything for me and looks after me so much. We've been friends for years. I never thought our friendship would last, but it has. He's a model who goes to the gym every day for hours on end. He looks after himself, and his body is so well sculpted ... yes, I've drooled about his body after 'accidentally' walking into the bath- room when he'd just got out of the shower. It's no coincidence that the door doesn't lock anymore. I really don't know how the lock got bent like that. I laugh to myself. Fifteen minutes of hard work that's how...

I get into my car, drive for ten minutes, and then get

out at the local school hall. I know I should walk, but that's too much like hard work. Fat Club is held every Monday evening. I try to go every week, but sometimes I just can't be arsed to be embarrassed anymore and then I'll give up. I pay ten euro for someone to tell me that I've put on weight, I've maintained my weight, or in rare circumstances, I've lost some weight.

Do you know how humiliating it can be?

No. Because you don't need to go to Fat Club. Let me tell you that, some weeks, I walk out of that school hall and I'm about two inches shorter than when I walked in.

Monday night is treat night. So, regardless of what the scales say, I always have a treat on a Monday night. Usually a Curly Wurly which has been in the freezer (making it last longer because it's harder to chew) or a cake, or something high in calories and *really* bad for me. Darragh usually buys me something, and we sit down together and eat in silence.

I've paid my money and I step up on the scales. "So, how do you think you did this week?" the girl behind the scales asks.

I know it's rude, but I don't know her name. I don't really want to know the name of the person who tells me week after week that I'm putting on weight and paying for the privilege.

"The week was good, but it's the weekends that I find hard. If only I could be weighed on a Thursday or a Friday then I'm sure it would be better," I moan, as I stand on the scales.

"Well done, Kayleigh. You've lost four pounds this week. Whatever you've done ... keep it up."

"Seriously? Let me get off and stand on them again. That can't be right." I step off the dreaded scales.

She laughs as she takes my card out and puts it back in

again. "Yeah, you've definitely lost four pounds. Well done!"

She writes down my loss and hands back my book and card. I step off and put on my socks, shoes, jewellery, glasses, and anything else I had taken off before I weighed myself.

Acknowledgments

There are always so many people who need acknowledgements when I write a book. Firstly, my Mum who reads all my books as soon as they are written. I also send her my first, rough, draft and get her opinion on whether I should publish or not. Thankfully, she loves the Mixology Series. Natasha, my PA, also gets my rough copy and tells me if I need to make any changes. Samantha Michelle Roberts has been added to the ladies that I trust with my first draft! Thank you my amazing alpha readers.

Jennifer Foster has been a fantastic support to me. We have become closer and life wouldn't be the same without her in it. She is an amazing friend, pamper and helps me to organise my life. Thanks babe.

As always my readers are so important to me and I thank each and every one of you for reading my books and enjoying them so much.

Love you lots like jelly tots Krissy V